WHAT I Lost, WHAT I Gained

JENNIFER R. LYONS

I would like to acknowledge all the parents out there
who tirelessly love.

Sitting there, in that beautiful theatre, I wondered how someone could hear such music from their own mind. I thought of how many great compositions the world has and the process of hearing noise, clearing it, feeling the peace over and again. Did they only experience blissful silence after daring to expunge it? No wonder so many of the greats were believed to be crazy. A smile crossed my face as I realized I can't even cope with two hours of noise after lunch with my two toddlers, even though I had been told, over and again, how the sound of children was true music. Honestly, it normally sounded like a lot of chaos and work. *When the composer hears a new ballet or opera forming in their minds is it born from chaos,* my overthinking mind was certainly not allowing me to enjoy my one precious evening out this month. I sighed and tried again. I closed my eyes briefly and allowed the beautiful music to wash over me.

Normally, gaining control through a deep breath is all it took to clear my thoughts. I felt renewed deep down in my soul. I opened my eyes, disappointed to find my partner watching me closely. *She knows*, I thought desperately, *It shows on my face, in my tired eyes*. I took her hand and forced my eyes forward, faking a beautiful smile full of warmth that felt far-removed from my day-to-day reality.

My hands were cold, my heart was empty, and not even the beautiful display of perfected art could dazzle me tonight. I glanced at her again, of course, she looked marvelous; all smart in her black trousers and jacket. Her hair was perfect, something I'd noticed when I first met her so long ago. It was always perfect. No matter how humid or windy, her hair was perfect. After each intense lovemaking session, she only had to shake her head and that hair returned to its natural, perfect-resting place. I felt my own jaw tighten just a little. My own hair had always taken time and upkeep and after the two babies, it was unpredictable and unmanageable. I tried to quell envy that pushed into my heart. Her hair was perfect, her tummy was tight. Her breasts, though small, were perfectly round and firm. No stretch marks, no tired circles under her eyes. Nothing to signify motherhood at all. I knew I looked her complete opposite.

She had always been beautiful. Now and especially by my side, she looked even more beautiful and glamorous. I wondered if she noticed or how much she cared. She didn't stay on because I was such fun; that simply wasn't me anymore. I suppose you could say I'd matured. I was no filled with safety concerns, activity dates, laundry, weekly menus, and tips on how to clean the toughest stains from any fabric. I wasn't militant but our home ran smoothly; any fifties housewife would have been proud. The years had etched into my face, into my soul.

My long hair was streaked with gray and it was flat. There was no sheen, no bounce. It was like my tired soul reflected through my hair. My eyes were constantly shadowed with dark circles and there were tiny lines around my mouth from years of practicing a disappointed silence. My former life was hardly even in a tangible memory in my heart anymore and nothing about me signified anything other than "Mom." Mom jeans were comfier than others, thanks to the strained muscles of having that parasitic life inside me for nine months, twice. My shoes were flat, reasonable, and ready to chase any escaping tiny person or soccer ball. My nails were short and clean. I didn't wear jewelry. I'd given up that habit the first year with Jordan, our first-born. It hurt to have earrings pulled and I didn't like him sucking on my necklaces. I no longer wore make-up day-to-day, saving that time-grabbing chore for only important dates out, which were fewer and fewer between now that our children were getting older.

Even though I laughed out loud, my soul seemed to shed tears almost continuously as I lost more and more of myself to this life. I forced myself back into the present, which was actually nearly perfect. I was sitting with the love of my life, watching a beautiful expression of music, dance, and costume. For once, I even felt I looked nice and the woman sitting there, holding my hand, looked wonderful. She put her other hand protectively over mine and smiled gently into my eyes. She wanted the best life for me. And I understood that for this moment, all the imperfections of my confinement could melt away. I listened to the music and forced all the non-sense from my mind. Nothing else mattered. For a little while, my soul breathed.

After that date night, life quickly returned back to normal. She got up early each morning to catch her train to her office further downtown. Perfect make-up, perfect hair, literally running out the front door, quiet enough to let the children sleep as long as possible. She kissed me on my cheek, told me she was happy to let me sleep in, and was gone.

I was glad to sleep in actually. I had been tired lately and sleep was one of my only comforts. Mostly, all I wanted was to forget all my responsibilities and sleep soundly. As I drifted off, I thought of how often I felt this way and even though that frightened me, I gave in to the sweet, peaceful, dreamless slumber my soul so desperately craved. I wanted nothing more from life.

2

A week or so after the show, I found myself doing the food shopping mid-morning on a rare outing alone. I had the ever-present list ordering me from one errand to the next, the week's menu, and the items needed to run our household. I never deviated from these lists. Our budget of both resources and time didn't allow for any deviations.

I hadn't always been like this. Before the lists ordered my life, I did food shopping only when needed. I bought what I wanted and if it went to waste, there were few repercussions. Going from two incomes to one demanded sacrifice. That sacrifice had not been easy though swift. Those lists were key to running an efficient, happy household. They capitalized both time and money. While I prided myself on such efficiency, deep down, I despised their creation and the power they held over my entire life.

I glanced at the list again. Today, I needed to run by the chemist to refill our stock of pain relievers; adult and children. I needed to run in to pay a bill on the bedroom suite we had recently purchased. The list was so complete I had even annotated there were only three more payments for the suite. I sighed for the thousandth and oneth time that day and saw her. It was only a reflection, so I looked to my left for the real person.

The woman had been pretty, at least at one time in her life. Her long hair was loose, graying, lank, and thin. It looked clean but unkept. She didn't wear any make-up. Not even lip gloss. Her hands were clean with clean, short nails. Her shoes were non-descript sneakers, not new but not in bad repair either. Her jeans were a little snug, especially on her tummy. Her coat was knee-length, gray, and open, revealing a simple black shirt. Her arms were full of her shopping. Clutched in one hand was an all-powerful list. There was no shine in her eyes. She glanced at her list and reached into the freezer to grab the next demanded item. Then she turned and slowly walked away. She didn't acknowledge me. I doubted she saw me, even though she very nearly ran into me.

Catching my own reflection in the space that previously held hers, I realized, aside from the color of the clothing, we could have been twins. I stared and stared. An empty woman stared back.

When had I become this? I, somehow, found my way to the front of the store where I paid, mumbled thanks, and stepped out into cool, fresh air. I was almost panicking as I tried to suck in as much air as my lungs could hold. My heart still pounded. I stumbled across the car park, and put the groceries into my car. I got in the driver's seat, carefully buckled my belt, and put the car in gear. Then I did what was necessary. I drove home, to the life I had so meticulously created.

Walking in, I felt my heart was calmer but I couldn't get the image of that other woman out of my mind. What had driven us to this point? I wanted to cry, I wanted to think and solve this riddle; I wanted to save myself. At that moment, the sitter left and the baby started crying. I glanced at my list, saw what was for lunch this Tuesday and did just as it ordered. We ate and I put her down for a nap. I was so tired, so I lay on the couch allowing that comfort of not thinking, not planning, not doing to wash over me, saving my drowning soul once again. I didn't wake until I heard the front door.

I glanced at the list to see what was planned for dinner.

The days went by with no change, even after such a revelation. I followed the list and slept, all that I could. I made more lists, allowing everyone else to be as happy and free as they deserved. I made all their favorite foods and took them to all their favorite places. Every time Chloe begged attention, I set aside whatever menial chores I was attending and listened or waited on whatever she needed. I was caught in a desperate whirl of mundane activity, though none of it fed my spirit. My only solace and escape were to sleep.

One Thursday during March, I looked out my front windows, out into the street. I saw a car passing. I felt that car was life and it was passing me by. Turning away from the window, I looked around at my beautiful home but felt like a prisoner. I hated the image of spoiled housewives and had worked so hard to overcome becoming that. Sarah worked outside our home and I… Even though, I probably matched her hard-work ethic, it was difficult, if not impossible, to feel differently. I decided it was time for a change. I joined a young mother support group.

Every Monday morning, the group met at a local church in the basement. Toys were provided for the children and one mother acted as leader. I couldn't believe how difficult walking in that first Monday was; my heart pounded and of course, Chloe cried. Jordan begged to go home the minute we got through the door. He wrapped himself around one of my legs and Chloe the other. God help me, I tried. I tried taking them to the other children, tried giving them their snacks, their drinks. I tried introducing myself. No other mums said much though and no one offered a kind word. As I looked around the group, I realized this was first thing on all our lists for the week. Everyone was just a little too empty to really befriend another new empty friend. I finally got up and gave quiet excuses and left.

I felt so sad leaving that place. I felt so defeated, yet, I didn't know how to stay. I certainly didn't want to interrupt the sanctity the others obviously had worked so hard to create. I wanted to be part of something outside my own making but didn't know how. By the time I got back home, a whole hour and half after venturing out, I'd decided I wasn't giving up. I looked at my list and found Monday's lunch. I sat the kids to the table and googled help for young mothers. I read all afternoon, right up until I heard the front door. Then, I found Monday's dinner on my list.

After my desperate search that Monday, I tried to implement the tips that I'd found. I was in danger of experiencing burn-out. I felt a little better knowing what it was. There were literally thousands of ways to overcome burnout. One was to implement self-care. I had to look up what that meant and came across a blog with what looked like great ideas. I carefully penciled in "me time" on each Wednesday evening from seven to nine. Later, I made sure Sarah understood what this meant; she was totally on board.

"You know, I've been thinking you need some time. I see you with the kids are always wrapped around you," she looked at me over the brim of her water glass at dinner that night, "And you are wrapped around them."

"I know, I know. I just…I don't know what to do without them. It's weird, they weren't here, then there were these amazing people we created and I can't think anything else. You know?" I watched her carefully, we had taken such different approaches to motherhood; it was a little strange. I could tell she didn't really get what I was saying. And how could she? I had been the one to carry the babies. It was me who labored through night and day to bring them into the world. She thought of everything outside our family, while I could think of little else.

"The thing is, Jess, you are a great mom. You really are and I am so grateful to the sacrifices you have made bringing them into this world. I see your body, how you try to hide what you call your "mum tum," I notice you never take your bra off. I watch you look away from the mirror when you get out of the shower. You rise with the kids and go after each day as if you are battling some great army. That is how much energy you use each day raising our babies. And I love you so much for it. I hope I give the same love I see you give. It's beautiful. But," she took another sip and met my eyes, "You are losing yourself to us. I see that more and more each day."

I couldn't look her in the eye, my chin fell forward and my eyes filled with tears. I was so ashamed. We'd been through hell when we'd decided to conceive. The mockery thrown our way, finding a donor, not only once but twice. Her family refused to talk with us or acknowledge our children. My own mom had been great support, so happy to be a grandmother. She was talking about moving closer but had died just a few months after Chloe was born. An aneurism had struck right after a visit. After enduring all that, here I was lost in the throes of living in a beautiful home, mostly provided by my lovely hard-working wife I was feeling envious towards. I felt so, so much despair and shame.

Who was I to feel this way? What more could life give me? Was I so empty, so shallow I couldn't even be grateful for with that with which I'd been so blessed? What more could I possibly even want? I was the one who'd dreamt of this life. All I'd wanted was to be a mum and wife. When I met Sarah, I'd told her of my dreams a few months into our relationship. She'd told me she'd never felt the same. As our relationship grew more and more serious, she'd given it more thought and finally, when she popped the question, she'd also whispered, "I can't wait to have babies with you." Just thinking of that moment, still made my skin tickle. I had it all. She was a great provider; we had a big home with a garden. She loved me, I knew it. I could feel it every time she looked at me. Every time she took my hand, I felt her love for me. I had beautiful children. "How dare I possibly feel anything but contented happiness?" I wondered for what felt like the millionth time.

How could I lose myself to something I'd desired and created?

The first "me time" Wednesday, I woke up feeling an excitement and for some unconscious reason, dread. I knew tonight was the night for me to begin taking care of myself, and now the list demanded it. I'd allotted two whole hours. What was I going to do for two hours? I googled self-care ideas. The first thing on the list was a bubble bath. I added "clean the bath tub" to the list and made the kids breakfast.

It took all day to prepare for my two hours. First, I made sure dinner was done and did the extra dishes. At least I wouldn't have to do them after we ate. I put the kids down for their afternoon nap. I made sure they went down right on time. If we were too early or late, Chloe's bedtime got all messed up. We went to the park and when we got home, I bathed them. Normal days, they bathed after dinner. I didn't want to put too much on Sarah after working. I cleaned the tub.

I set the table for dinner. I put books by their beds. Sarah wouldn't even have to look. I even made sure there was wine for Sarah for after she put the kids down.

I put her favorite magazine on the couch. Even though the list demanded "me time," it didn't designate "Jess time." I certainly didn't want to take away from Sarah's night. After all, she'd been working all day.

When she got home, she was carrying flowers. She kissed my cheek and looked around the house, surprised. "Jesus, Jess, you've been busy! Are you going away for a few days?"

I laughed, "No, no. I was just going to take a bath and read tonight. I wanted you to have an easy night, too." I tried looking around the house with her eyes.

Our home was normally tidy. We both liked it that way and we were already teaching our children to tidy up as well. Every weekend, we deep-cleaned one day and went out the other. Today, the house literally shone from my extra efforts; especially for a Wednesday. I felt a little silly, I'd thought I was doing her a favor, making her night with the children easier. My heartbeat a little faster. Anxiously, I asked if it was too much.

"No, you never do too much. It's lovely you did all this for us tonight," and she kissed my cheek.

We ate and she shooed me out of the kitchen even before the list's designated time of seven o'clock, reminding me she could clean a few plates as well as me.

I walked into the bathroom and carefully closed and locked the door. Locking the door was Sarah's idea. She'd pointed out if I was staying home, the kids would want tonight to be like any other and Jordan could open the doors. She had been just as thoughtful preparing for tonight, too. Headphones were on the vanity along-side already burning candles. I drew myself a bath. I undressed, avoided the reflection in the mirror, and got in.

The bath was sheer luxury. Lots of warm water enveloped my body. The bubbles were softly fragrant. Best of all, I couldn't hear anything but the beautiful piano music pouring into my headphones. My body was warm, the bath salts relaxing, and I tried really hard not to over-think anything. Every time my mind thought about what needed to happen next, I forced myself not to dwell. I lay completely still and un-thinking.

After what felt a long time but surely was only a few minutes, I realized this was my first bath alone since I'd had Chloe. I was always getting in the shower with Sarah or one of the kids inevitably walked in. I hadn't taken the time for even a shower or bath on my own in over a year. The thought made me a little sad. I reflected on an article I'd come across the last month or so.

It was on the duties of motherhood. It reminded mothers children were constantly growing, and we can't hold back time. All those little handprints wouldn't be possible in a few short years. It advised us to enjoy the precious present. Anyone can put up with a few short years of crying and need. This time doesn't last and it pointed out how lucky we were to experience it. I recalled it ending with something like 'Look around. How many friends do you have, right now, who desperately wanted children but are unable? How can you even dare complain when you have such a blessing each day?' I felt ashamed, first for needing some time and then for enjoying it.

My next thoughts were all on the article. How right it was, this time was such a blessing that not everyone gets to experience. My god, look at how many babies are lost to miscarriage or still birth? Look at how many tragic accidents families endure each year, losing their precious babies that were once so tenderly? Even Sarah and I had fought to conceive, though not as hard or as long as some of our friends. My pregnancies were normal. I'd experienced the normal morning sickness the first trimester. Both deliveries had gone well. I hadn't even needed stitches. I breathed that lavender in and reminded myself of just how lucky I was.

As the water grew cold, I carefully got out, avoided the reflection in the mirror, and toweled off. I even dried my hair with the hair dryer. I put a soft robe around me and quietly walked to our room. Sarah was asleep on her side of the bed. I snuggled in beside her and went to sleep without one struggle. Right before I drifted off, I reminded myself to be grateful for all I had.

Each week, I looked forward to my Wednesday evenings. All day Wednesday, I would clean and ready for my night out that I actually spent in. I took my bath and did a little reading. Sarah never once complained or worked late those evenings. It was a simple but wonderful gesture.

I also tried going back to the support group on Mondays. Instead of just giving into my children's demands, I stayed my ground and really enjoyed the meetings. Eventually, Jordan and Chloe joined the other children and gave me some space to enjoy some adult company. It was a safe space to employ child language and adult language simultaneously; after all, we were all in the same boats of motherhood.

I learned a little about each woman in the group over the next month or so. No one else was in a lesbian relationship but no one acted as if that were a problem. They talked about their husbands, laughing about the differences between male and female brains once in a while. I laughed, too. One nice woman, her name was Beth, did ask one day how Sarah and I managed the household, was it comparable to everyone else's experience?

I'd laughed and asked, "Do you mean is she the man and I the woman?" I glanced around and noticed everyone was a little nervous but curious, too. I went on, "No, I don't think it actually goes that way because, you see, I was never attracted to men. Perhaps, it was because of the differences between males and females' brains. We do experience the same issues though. And you know? I am a little surprised by that."

A woman named Kim asked, "Like what? I just figured your house was clean, all the time with everything in their places, schedules kept, you know, because you probably think the same?" Her cheeks reddened a little but she went on, "I mean, I don't want to discredit you, but it is really difficult being married to a man who just doesn't get it. I work hard all day, keeping our home up, raising our children, and he acts like he is in on everything. And most of the time, he's not. Not even close. In fact, a lot of the time, I feel as if I am picking up after him more than I do the kids!"

At those words, every single woman nodded their ascent.

"I just figured that was how a man thinks, or doesn't think," Beth chimed in again, "Most of the time, he doesn't even notice he never has to look for anything, do his own wash, or even think about what is for dinner. Do you struggle with that, too?"

Before I could answer, a woman who went by a nickname, Skip, put her thoughts in, "You know, maybe we were wrong. Maybe, because we are home, they just sort of take advantage of all we do. Like, no matter if we are married to a man or woman, whomever stays home just does everything there and the other doesn't think about it. You know though, I work thirty hours a week, and I still do all this. It's not like he's working sixty hours, he only works about forty. And I still do all this."

Every face turned towards me. I hadn't really expected this. All I could do was speak what I knew, "Well, Sarah, that's my wife's name, her and I do think quite a lot the same on how to run our home. We both like it clean and we both want the children to have a sense of order. I guess, we have fallen into certain roles as we have added to our family. I do most of the meal planning and cooking. And running the kids around. And planning our house hold errands. I plan every day around everyone else. And even on my nights out, I work really hard so Sarah doesn't have to do much extra.

I make sure dinner is finished and the kids are bathed before she even gets home those evenings. I make sure the extra dishes are finished so all she has to do is put the plates and such into the dishwasher. I even put the books by the kids' beds so she doesn't have to retrieve them. I leave out her favorite wine and magazine so she can relax a little, too."

"Okay, I hear you saying you do most of the home running but does Sarah *notice?* Because, Mark, God knows how much I love him, he does not notice. Ever," that was Beth again.

A few other joined in then and I never answered. I was thinking of something Sarah said a few weeks ago one Wednesday. She looked forward to "me time" as much as me. She enjoyed putting the kids down a little early and just being herself. The words hadn't meant much at the time, but now, I wondered if she knew how much work I put into each Wednesday. I was pretty sure she did notice and even appreciated all I was doing. That statement even affirmed it. The real question was did I.

That night, at dinner, I told her about some of the conversation at the Monday meeting. She nodded and sipped her wine while I rinsed the nightly dishes. She asked me the same question, "Do you think I notice?"

I answered her with a kiss. I wrapped my arms around her and pulled her close, enjoying the feeling of her warmth and beauty next to me. I kissed her top lip, then her bottom lip, and finally her tongue while stroked her perfect hair. When I ended it, she pulled back, just a little and whispered, "Good, because, Jess, I love you. I never want you to think I don't notice all you do here."

My heart felt full but, of course, I hadn't dared answered the question for myself.

4

The next weeks went by in much the same blurry fashion as always. I made my lists, ran around, and was careful to take my "me time" each Wednesday night. On one of those Tuesdays, I'd noticed spring was thankfully on its way in and the kids and I had made a list to begin planting our seeds the next few days. "You can't eat the seeds, Chloe," Jordan had told his sister. She was too little to understand but her big eyes took in everything Jordan told her. He was a good big brother.

I told Sarah about their little exchange over dinner. I absolutely loved watching my children growing up. Recalling it, I laughed and Sarah smiled. I asked Sarah how her day was and she'd responded with something like it was alright until she'd gone to the gym.

I was surprised. I hadn't known she was going to the gym. I asked her when she went.

"I go every day, Jess. Just as I've always done, I never stopped," her simple answer stopped me in my tracks.

I'd no idea Sarah had kept up with her gym workouts. After I had Jordan, I hadn't set foot in a gym. I looked over at my wife who was now holding Chloe in her lap. I was extremely hurt, but I wasn't sure why. To hide my hurt, I did what most housewives have done for centuries, I started doing the evening chores.

As I cleared the table, I looked over at my wife and children. Sarah had removed them from the table and gone to the living room. She was on the living room floor, playing with them, tickling Chloe's tummy and rolling Jordan around on the floor. I'd always wondered at her energy in the evenings. Now, I understood where she got it from, she worked out.

Fitness had been very important to both of us when we'd first met. Sarah was more into as the years went by and when I'd gotten pregnant with Jordan, my O.B. had suggested gentle, long walks, instead of weights or even heavy cardio because I was carried him so low. Once I'd had him, it was nearly impossible to fit in gym time with his feedings and all. Then we had Chloe. I had tried to go, but that hadn't lasted. Sarah never offered or asked why I stopped going. I did walk a lot. Always with the kids in tow or with a stroller. My heart actually hurt with the realization Sarah had somehow kept up with the gym. Where did she get the time?

"So, you went to the gym? When?" I casually called out.

"I go every day for about an hour or so. You know my company gives me time," she'd called back. Her and the kids were really laughing.

No, I hadn't known that actually, I resentfully thought to myself. For some reason, the thought brought tears to my eyes. What a pair we must make. There was Sarah, so fit, so young looking. She never skipped the gym. She never skipped a hair appointment either. I hadn't gotten mine even trimmed since before Chloe. I looked out again at the three of them.

There was her beautiful, trim figure. Her face, even in this relaxed setting, exuded self-confidence. I noticed she was wearing her favorite color, a peachy color that made her skin glow. I honestly couldn't recall what my own favorite color was right then or what colors made my skin glow. I was wearing jeans and a faded, gray t-shirt; safe clothes that fit into any chore or activity the kids and I did.

"You can go anytime, you know," I hadn't noticed Sarah was standing beside me now, "I don't mind. I thought maybe you didn't like going anymore? Or maybe you just wanted to continue the walks?"

She was really studying my face.

I didn't know how to answer her. What was it I wanted? Did I want to go to the gym? Or keep up with the walking? I wasn't sure. I didn't know what I wanted. I felt bad to even feel that displaced hurt and envy.

I smiled, forcing my array of feelings down, "Oh, I don't know. I'll figure it." She patted my shoulder and walked back to the living room. I felt so dumb and isolated.

There I was and I couldn't figure out what my own favorite color was. I couldn't decide if I wanted to take a simple walk or go to the gym. I looked at the list. There was no time for the gym or a walk.

I could vividly recall what it was like going to the gym with the babies though. I certainly didn't want *that.* Even with the child care provided, it had been difficult. I'd had to pack the diaper bags, ready Jordan and Chloe, then ignore their wails as I ducked into a room busy with really fit people. I'd waddled over to the elliptical, feeling as if my stretched-out tummy was on naked display for everyone to see. As soon as I'd worked up a good sweat, one of the care-givers ran over to tell me Chloe had a blow-out. Every time had gone that way, for the entire month, I'd tried it until I couldn't bear it any longer. I hadn't lost an ounce of the baby weight. I wasn't getting any firmer and with all the interruptions, it wasn't worth it. I watched my family playing together for a moment. Sarah had never brought the children to the gym, after all, she went during work hours. She couldn't know how difficult that had been.

Making a bold decision, I penciled a new task on my list, "gym time." I would go for an hour each afternoon when Sarah got home from work. I could do that and Sarah seemed happy with the idea when I told her later. I decided to start the very next day.

It happened to be a Wednesday, so busy day, getting ready for "me time" and "gym time." I still didn't want to bother Sarah with more work, so I readied the house for the evening. We normally ate soon after Sarah walking in the door, so I gave the kids a late snack to hold them over then I'd be at the gym. That way, I could be home to eat with them and of course, I could also clean up. Sarah worked all day after all. I put dinner in the oven on my out the door and high-fived Sarah on her way in.

I wore yoga pants which kept my mommy pouch tucked in a little. I got on that elliptical and really tackled the workout but about eight minutes in, I realized how out of breath I was. I slowed my pace and tried to ignore the reflection watching me. I finished thirty minutes on that machine and decided to do some light weights. I finished the hour workout and headed back home.

I took dinner out of the oven and served everyone. Sarah looked gorgeous, making me wonder how she did it. We both did workouts but here I was all sweaty in my gym clothes, and there she was, clean. I asked her about it.

"I always shower at the gym, silly. I don't want to drive home all sweaty. I just dry my hair and all while I'm there," she smiled and patted my knee. I nodded in return but couldn't smile or meet her eyes.

I had rushed right home after my workout. It hadn't even dawned on me to shower or do anything else while I was away.

I had stuff to do this evening and couldn't be away more than necessary. I felt a little hollow, though. Sarah worked out every day. And showered and did her hair every day at the gym. How long did all that take? I wondered.

After dinner, per our now usual Wednesday night ritual, I cleared up the few remaining dishes and snuck upstairs for my bath. I had to clean out the tub first. Then, Jordan knocked, "Mommy, I just really like how you read this story, can you read tonight?"

I nodded and left the bathroom.

Sarah took Chloe and I read to Jordan. It was a lovely time for just him and me. I read and he listened right to the end. I told him how much I loved him and how proud he made us each day. He asked about planting the seeds. I told him we would do that in the morning and kissed his forehead and left his room.

Sarah asked if I wanted to have a glass of wine. I accepted. It was so nice to have an impromptu glass of wine in the middle of the week. What a treat!

That was the end of "me time" on Wednesdays. I never again put them on the list.

I did keep up my new gym routine. Sarah didn't seem to notice I had stopped the Wednesday "me time." Or maybe, she just figured I had replaced it with my gym time. Whatever she thought, she didn't ask and I didn't ask for any time again. Life was just too busy.

I was exhausted more than ever. Since I was now going to the gym, every afternoon, I got dinner ready and readied the kids as much as I could every single day, so Sarah could relax more after her working all day. She never questioned this but did thank me here and there. When I stopped taking "me time" Wednesdays, she stopped bringing flowers, too.

I never thought to question why or how much I was doing as I ran around doing it all. Sarah and I high-fived as we ran in and out and chased the babies.

I was glad for the business. The busier I was, the less I thought. And the more sleep engulfed me each night as I sought solace from my well-planned life and all the lists.

5

A couple of months seemed to just fly by and the kids and I planted our seedlings outside in a warm-ish sun. They loved it. They loved getting dirty and being outside after winter. Chloe took a long, long nap and was still asleep when Sarah and I high-fived my way to the gym. It was a Wednesday.

When I got home, Sarah met me at the door, sipping a glass of wine. I could hear Chloe wailing in the house. "She woke up, just a few minutes ago, I have no idea what to do. I think she wants you," she told me as I went in. I went to take the glass from her and she held onto it, "Oh, do you want some? I can do that," and she whisked away to the kitchen, leaving me empty handed and to care for a wailing toddler.

I picked up my precious girl and brought her close to my heart. Her sobbing subsided as I walked into the kitchen to retrieve dinner from the oven. Sarah met me halfway. She was now holding two glasses. "I really don't need any right now, thanks. Can you just grab dinner from the oven, please?" I asked. She nodded and did so. I called Jordan and sat down at our table with Chloe on my lap and Jordan climbing into his own chair. Sarah asked what to do next.

I looked at her out of the corner of my eye, "I normally fill the plates over there and then bring them to the table." I said that out loud, but inside, *How can you not know this?*

Chloe wasn't crying anymore but she was doing that hiccup breathing thing, so I wasn't ready to put her down just yet. Sarah filled each plate and brought them over to the table. Then, she got our wine glasses.

"Why did you ask me what to do with dinner?" I was curious. It wasn't that difficult. After all, we had done the same thing most every day for the past two years. Dinner was cooked, the extra pots and pans were cleaned, what more could there possibly be to do other than just eat?

"Oh, I don't know, Jess, I guess I just got stressed with the baby howling like that. Then, Jordan wouldn't stop asking me to see the plants and I just got a little overwhelmed," she took another sip of wine.

I guess I couldn't understand. I was the one to constantly soothe crying toddlers, entertain them, clean up after them, clean them, feed them, and all the rest. What could she mean she got overwhelmed? I'd only been gone a little over an hour. A deep breath kept my temper in check.

We made small talk and I got the kids ready for their bath. Sarah certainly did not look like she was in a mood to do that, so I cleared the table and whisked the kids upstairs. Sarah stayed down with another glass of wine and stretched out, feet up with her favorite magazine. I decided she must have had a rough day at work. I bathed the kids and got them ready for bed. I tucked them each in and kissed their foreheads.

I went downstairs to check on Sarah, to see how her day was, still in need of a shower. She told me they were in the middle of a new project and it was stressful. She explained there were a couple new people on the team. One had been a stay at home mom for a few years and just getting back into the game. Sarah told me she seemed nice but really scattered. I tried not to think what that meant or how much life had altered my once clear thought process. She finished her little rant and sat back, breathing deeply.

I wondered what she really thought of her new team member.

"At least the gym was good, I started a new spinning class."

She didn't say anything else, didn't ask how I was or how my day was. So, I began telling her and she picked up her magazine. She wasn't reading it, I could tell but her focus certainly wasn't on the kids and I either.

"You know, today is Wednesday," I finally said.

"Right, I know, Jess. I always know what day a week it is."

"Just a few weeks ago, I started self-care," I reminded her. She sighed and put her magazine down.

"So, I am a jerk for not remembering tonight?" her voice was so hard.

It had been a long time since our last fight. I couldn't remember the last time we had spoken harshly back and forth.

"It's not that, Sarah. But it has been several weeks since I did my Wednesday night stuff."

She sighed, "I just figured you had stopped that since you were going to the gym."

"So, I can't have both? You do," I was getting angrier and more hurt by the second.

"What do you mean I have both. Since when?" she demanded.

I couldn't believe I had to answer. I pointed out her hair appointments, her daily gym time, how she showered alone, and how the house and the chores were finished each day so I could feel like I could venture out for a one-hour workout.

"I don't make you do any of that," she pointed out. Then, she got up and went to bed.

I sat; stunned into silence.

She was right. I was the one who had appointed myself to all the chores, all the care-giving. I'd given myself that role; no one else had assigned it. I cried. I felt so bad, blaming Sarah and just all of it. I felt so alone. All I did was chase everyone around, trying to squeeze an hour into the gym each day that even after a month wasn't paying off.

I slept on the couch that night. She left without saying goodbye. Or at least, I think she left without saying goodbye. She didn't wake me if she'd tried.

The next day, I got a long text from Sarah around mid-morning. She said she was sorry I was losing myself to motherhood but that she hoped I realized I was doing this to myself. She wasn't keeping me from hair appointments or the gym. She didn't care if the house was clean or not. Or if we had four course nightly meals. She just wanted me to be happy again and she understood how unhappy I had been.

I tried to sort out my feelings. And I didn't go to the gym that day.

The thing was, I did understand I had given myself the role of primary caretaker. After all, I was the one who carried the babies. I was the one who delivered them into the world. I was the one who wanted to be a mother. I was happy being a mother. And a wife. I was even thankful for everything we had. I just didn't know myself very well. I couldn't think outside my little family. I cooked nightly meals not solely for enjoyment, but for nutrition. I wanted our children to grow healthy and strong. We needed good nutrition, too.

I think and I thought that day, surely, most housewives go through this stage. We lose ourselves, a little to our art and at some point, we have to fight to figure out our core identity again. We give up everything for our babies, beginning with our bodies. Most of us are only too happy to do all we can for those we cherish most.

Sarah was a great mother and a great wife. She just took a different approach to life. I paled in comparison to her professionally. She had always made more than me. She dared ask for raises and had gotten most of them. She'd worked hard for each promotion. I was so proud of her. She would never lose herself to another person, not even her children because she was so confident at *being* Sarah.

I was a great mother and wife, too. I never possessed her bold nature and possibly because of that, my professional career had been only alright. I certainly couldn't afford the home we lived in, nor the clothes we bought our children. If I was honest to myself, I'd lost a bit of myself willingly to her before we even had children. She hadn't asked that from me and she certainly never demanded it. No, I had done so willingly, blinded by her sheer beauty inside and out. If I was honest, I was a little sad she hadn't been as dazzled by me.

At any rate, once I had lost a little of myself to her, it was no wonder I had given so much of myself away to our children. I'd told myself that was demanded of a good mother, but my own wife was example of how wrong that thinking was. And yet, why hadn't she noticed all I was doing for us, why hadn't she cared to see what was happening to me, to step in, to stop it?

In the ten years we had known each other, Sarah was pretty much the same. Her ideals were the same, her looks hadn't really changed, and her demeanor was exactly the same. She paid attention to current fashion. Sure, she was a little older, a little wiser, but not *changed.*

I had aged. I wore different clothes now; my hair was just long that was most often tied up in the back. I was quieter, even less bold than before. I didn't look people in the eye like I had before. I didn't initiate conversation. At the last office family day, I cared for the kids while Sarah greeted everyone, then talked with everyone. I had spoken only when spoken to. I'd always been shy, but this was something more. Having children had changed me, for sure. And I wasn't sure it was for the better.

Even amongst these thoughts, trying to save myself, the articles of child-rearing came back to haunt me, warning me to be grateful for a short time I was a mum to growing children. Each stage only lasts a few months, each age a year, and each precious moment is fleeting. Looking around my own home, I felt ashamed. Not everyone lived in such a safe, beautiful place. Our own home was furnished with nice, comfy, inviting furniture. It wasn't glamorous but it was beautiful. How could anyone who got to stay here each day, all day ever feel anything but grateful?

I went to the bathroom and locked the door. I collapsed to the floor, sobbing, wishing there was someone, anyone I could ask what I was supposed to do next. I missed my mom. I wondered if she'd ever experienced this stage. I wished Sarah could understand what I was going through. Soon enough, Chloe's little fingers were reaching under the door, out to me. It was time to stop this stupid self-wallowing and do what needed to be done. I wiped my eyes and got up off the floor. I picked Chloe up and checked the list for Thursday lunch.

I didn't go to the gym that day either. In fact, I stopped going altogether.

I decided to focus all my energy on my growing family. I resolved this was a short time in life and once these days, these weeks, these precious months were gone, I would never get them back. I did keep up with the Monday meetings, laughing with the other mommies over our daily struggles. And I pushed Jess down further and further, trying to stomp out any of her desires or dreams or resentment. I assured myself over and again this time was quickly passing.

Shifting my focus seemed to help. Sarah took me out for our monthly dates and we enjoyed some of the most beautiful outings offered in our city. We had a nice time together, just like always and we didn't argue. I raised our babies, acknowledging to be grateful for each day I spent with them. Only briefly did I wonder what I would do with myself when they grew and my role would change once again.

Sarah made sure to compliment me each day no matter how I looked. She told me I was beautiful, she craved me in bed, and she thanked me for raising my babies. I convinced myself I was really living the best life I ever could, ever would. And the years flew by.

Ten years flew by.

6

"Go, Jordan! Run! Get it! Yes!" I cheered madly for the handsome young man I proudly called son. He was a great player, very athletic, probably most thanks to Sarah's dedication to fitness. He ran with easy coordination. He was a delight to watch. I was awed at the young man down on the field. He was taller than me and the hint of peach fuzz was on his chin. He was quick and intelligent. Best of all, he was kind all the time. He wasn't a ball hog or arrogant, even though he was one of the best on the team.

After the game, I waited for him in the car park. We had to get Chloe from her swim practice. I brought snacks for him and he wolfed them down, the way boys do at his age. I ruffled his sweaty hair, not even minding the smell too much. We kept the windows down and I turned up his favorite song. A few minutes later, Chloe climbed in and we drove home.

Sarah had beat us home, she was waiting at the door. "Well? How was it?" she wanted to know before we were even out the car. Jordan ran up, hugged her, and told her all about the game, play by play. Chloe ran up, hugged her mother, and the three entered the house. I retrieved all the equipment and put it away in the garage before going inside.

The house smelled great. I'd put dinner in the crockpot before I'd left that morning. I breathed in the smell and my stomach gurgled in response. Sarah gave me a quick kiss and told me how great it smelled. I served up four plates and we settled into dinner.

I really did have a gorgeous family I decided looking at the three of them. Chloe wasn't tall like her brother. Her dark eyes and light skin made her bright, blue eyes stand out. I always thought she looked more like a piece of art than human. Jordan was a great looking kid, short dark blond hair, dark brown eyes. Even though he'd just snacked in the car, he shoveled in the food. Sarah was beautiful and perfect as ever. Her body was still firm, topped with that perfect hair. It had a few strands of gray. Her eyes were shining at the what the kids were saying and she said she had some great news for us.

It seemed she'd earned yet another promotion. This one was different though. She'd bought some shares in the company a long time ago and now with what she'd earned this past two years and next, she would be able to retire in only twelve months. She wouldn't be going to work every day in only one short year. She poured her and I the champagne she'd brought home that I hadn't noticed until this moment.

I was stunned.

I was so proud of my beautiful wife. What more could I ever dream of having, ever? We toasted her and congratulated her. I couldn't believe it. I excused myself saying I needed the restroom.

I walked through our house, up the stairs, and I looked at each photograph displayed showing off all our precious, hard-won memories. There was Jordan at his first soccer game and Chloe in her first gymnastics class. A scene of Sarah getting promoted. The three of them on our first beach vacation. The four of us in front of a Christmas tree. All twenty years of life, right up there on our wall.

I am so proud of Sarah, I thought. I decided to have a bath.

"Me time" Wednesdays had never rematerialized but of course, the kids were nearly grown and I had more "me time" than I ever thought possible. *Except*, I thought as I leaned into the bathwater.

The thing was even though the kids were in school all day and clubs after, I didn't have all that much free time during the day. Every single day I got up, got breakfast ready, and ran the kids to school. It took forever. You would think the school was brand new every year, they changed the enter and exit at least two times a year. No one ever figured it out and it took longer than forty-five minutes each day to drop them off. Every single day.

By the time I got done with the school drop-off, I ran whatever errands demanded from the list. I picked up prescriptions, I picked up whatever groceries we needed, and at least two mornings a week, Chloe forgot something from home. I hardly ever actually sat down to eat lunch. Then, only two hours later, it was time to pick them up. Then, two more hours of clubs and practices and home again. Just in time to fix dinner.

On Tuesdays and Thursdays, I tried to get to the gym, and I tried to walk every morning. I made it a point to wear at least some make-up each day. As I got out of the bath, I forced myself to look at the reflection in the mirror. I still had the poochy, mommy tummy. Nothing had saved my boobs. My arms were a bit saggy. And the thigh gap was pretty much gone. My neck was getting wrinkles. I couldn't remember the last time I got my hair cut. I sighed and pulled on my robe.

I wondered how life would change when Sarah would retire. She came into our room and grabbed me around my waist, pulling me to her. She reached into my robe and fondled my chest a little. "We made it, Jess," Sarah's voice was soft, smooth. She pushed her face into my neck. And tipped me back onto the bed. I was so happy. For her.

I went to sleep feeling so lucky to have this amazing woman in my life who loved me for reasons I still couldn't fathom. As I fell asleep, my mind drifted to darker corners.

Lying there in the dark, my arms wrapped around my beautiful wife, my mind took over. I wondered why

Sarah still loved me. My body certainly had changed and not for the better. Most days, I felt like I was just barely keeping up with the needs and wants of our little family. My own goals and career ambitions were long forgotten and I doubted I would or could ever remember them.

From there, I reminded myself it was not only career goals that I'd forgotten about myself. My own home was decorated in a taste, a style that fed Sarah's desires and our family's needs. None of it reflected me. When I was younger, I had dreamt of a home filled with color. Sarah liked a more neutral home. She never told me what I like wasn't good enough, I'd simply wanted to please her, so I pushed my own style aside. She worked so hard, outside the home and too much color seemed to cause her stress.

I wondered over and again what my life would look like in a year. The kids loved Sarah so much. Sarah had always been working and it was a treat to have her around. They loved me, too, but I was always around. Always. Dependability is nice, but it's often under-appreciated.

At dinner, she had expressed the desires to bring them to school and attend their practices. She had even winked at me and told me I could stay home if I would rather, get away from some of that traffic I complained about so often. I had smiled back but my heart hurt at words meant to lift me up.

I knew my life had been spent chasing everyone, helping them realize their own goals, their own achievements. I felt appreciated but I was well-aware of the fact how menial my life truly was. Most of my day to day was doing the humble tasks life demanded that did not require much thought or expertise. Throughout the ages, service had been thrust first upon slaves, then hired staff. Most of what I did from love could be done by anyone.

That truth hit me harder than I'd expected. I actually felt pain course through my body.

I could never walk into Sarah's life and perform at the levels she did. But I could be replaced quickly by almost anyone. After years of chasing her corporate life, she could simply step in and take over all I'd ever done. My life's work was not worthless or unappreciated. But.

I had spent the better part of my thirties and now, forties doing chores. I felt a tear slide down one cheek. In that moment, I knew the truth of my life. I knew how much I was loved by a wife I felt undeserving to have. I knew how much she and our wonderful children appreciated me. I knew I was well-provided for and well-loved.

I could not comprehend why Sarah loved my increasingly saggy body. I could not comprehend why I was so loved by these three amazing people. Deep down, I even rejected some of their love. I could not see what there was to love. The realization of living a mundane life, of doing nothing remarkable with myself—ever— hurt. And as I realized these things more and more washed over my soul, convincing me I was worthless.

I hung onto my sleeping wife, silently sobbing into my pillow. I knew this year would end quickly and Sarah would step into her "home" shoes easily and swiftly. There would be no room for me, no need. I supposed I would need to do what I always did. The reality was my children were nearly grown. All the years of them needing me were nearly behind us; then what? Both would drive soon. Both did most of their own chores and laundry now. Both would leave. Soon.

I knew Sarah would find some amazing tasks to fill her days. She had often talked about serving our community in some way. She would start a non-profit, organize meals on wheels, change legislation, visit schools, and continue being her amazing self. I hadn't done any of those things, even though I was at home most days. I couldn't see myself doing them in my future.

In fact, I couldn't see my future at all. All I could see was what I had been doing was coming to a rather abrupt end. There was nothing moving forward. I had loved being a mother to our children. I loved it with every fiber of my being. There was nothing like waking up to my children's faces, kissing them, feeding them, and getting on with each day's activities with them. I loved serving my family. It was true, it was lonely, I had lost myself to them, but God, I loved them. When Jordan and Chloe moved on, I could not see any future for myself. There, the path grew dark.

The next few days are little more than a blur in my memories. I recall understanding I had entered some sort of depression. I realized I could not allow myself to dwell on all the realizations that somehow simultaneously brought me down and raised my anxiety. I realized the next big thing for me might be my own death. I had been existing for others so long, I was sure I couldn't live without them.

What's more, I didn't want to.

After all, what would a life without hearing Jordan's goofy laugh everyday even be like? I didn't want to think about living without Chloe under our roof, not kissing her cheek every morning. As I thought of what our family was facing, my heart hurt a lot. Instead of these thoughts coming and going as they do, mine looped around and around again. I saw Sarah, fit and beautiful, standing before a bunch of teens demonstrating self-defense. I saw Chloe engaged with the briefing, her eyes on her beautiful mom, ready to introduce her friends afterwards.

I saw Jordan, going off to some college. He was excited to leave, excited to begin his new adventures. Sarah was there, hugging him, cheering him on. I was there, too, organizing his cramped dorm room, knowing it would all be undone in a matter of hours.

I didn't want an empty life, living off of Sarah's good graces. Then a chilling realization hit me full force, causing me to take in a sharp breath.

I could no longer survive on my own.

Not because I would be lonely. Not because I was so in love with my wife or even my children. No, I am talking about basic survival. I couldn't support myself.

There was no way I could afford rent, a car payment, utilities, and food for myself. Whatever happened next in my life, financially speaking, was all on Sarah.

I had grown too old. Too much time between career goals existed. No matter what happened next, I was dependent on my wife to meet my needs. My simple day-to-day chores paled in comparison of such a price.

At some point, I resolved I would not allow myself to get any deeper in this depression. I called it "stupid" and "needless." I told myself I was being silly and too sensitive. Those were traits I had always struggled against. Instead of fixing myself long before, here I was at the age I was, face-to-face with the same demons. I called myself weak. I didn't dare tell Sarah, who was over the moon at planning our next chapter, any of my fears or misgivings. I did what I'd always done, push Jess down and checked out the list.

Chloe did ask me, one time, if I was alright. She said I was looking sad. I smiled and assured her I was fine and busied myself with some much needed vacuuming, all while talking worse and worse to myself. She gave me a hug and a glance that clearly said, "I don't believe you." I didn't want to burden my child though, so I gritted my teeth and smiled into her beautiful face.

Sarah was slowly taking over all our dinner times to plan our summer vacation. I really wanted to go to a resort we had visited a few years ago near the beach. I wanted to watch the kids in the surf and sit back in the warm sun doing nothing at all. When I mentioned that to the three of them, they wrinkled their noses and said, "Boring."

I supposed it *was* a bit boring, especially when Sarah brought up her plans of a luxurious cruise with stops in all these fantastic islands. She brushed my hair off my shoulder and showed me a brochure and it really did look lovely. She was excited and said, "Well, this is our one last time we really can plan a family vacation! Jordan is out the year after!"

They all laughed and cheered at the idea. I cleared the table, happy to see them all smiling, wondering why time had stolen my precious babies. I didn't contradict them with any of their planning. I didn't want to take away any of their joy.

A few Saturdays later, Sarah offered to take the kids to their events for the day.

"You deserve a break from all this, you know? I can take it from here."

The last little bit anyone really needed from me was taken. I didn't protest or ask for it back. I just smiled and nodded.

By the time they got home, the house was absolutely sparkling. I had cleaned more than I had in the last two years. My heart was happy. I was excited for them to come home to a welcoming home where no chores, no responsibilities awaited them for a few days. Finishing up the last bathroom, I decided we should go out for dinner.

They were a little later than I had hoped, but of course, I knew better than anyone what traffic could be like. I decided to shower before they got home. As I was getting out, I heard a shout.

"Mom brought us to dinner! We ate at the new Greek place! I love Greek food!" Chloe was so excited to tell me all about it. Apparently, both events had let out a little early and they had run over there to try it out.

"See? I can do whatever you need, my love," Sarah sweetly whispered in my ear. I smiled through my devastation. All day, all I'd wanted was to be near them, to eat with them, and I'd worked really hard to give us that time.

"You didn't have to clean! I was going to tackle that tomorrow!" Sarah pointed out the cleaned living room.

"Oh, I just, you know. I had some time," I mumbled the words.

Chloe and Jordan already had the T.V. turned on, "I did all the laundry, got it all finished. I thought maybe we could all just enjoy tomorrow a little more."

"Oh, no, did you check my pockets?" Sarah ran to the dryer, "I had some receipts I was saving for work in my trousers from yesterday. You know what? I can get the laundry next week, okay? Then, we just don't have to worry."

Jordan called out, "Yeah, the last time you washed my stuff, two shirts were shrunk. I can get mine, Mom, don't worry about it."

"Did you clean our rooms, too?" Chloe asked.

"Yes! I did both of them, I got all your laundry hung up, but I put your folded things on your beds."

"Oh, well, I guess, I'll be sleeping next to all that tonight. I don't want to do anything else, I am so stuffed!" Chloe laughed.

There I stood, my hands red and raw from all my scrubbing all day, hungry only to face the realization again of how I was no longer needed. In fact, it looked as if I'd somehow dented their perfect day.

I wasn't feeling hungry anymore. I walked to the stairs to go take a bath. As it was filling up, Sarah came in, "Nice, I was hoping you would rest tonight. I only want to make your life good, you know that?"

She took my hand while she spoke.

I did know that but at this moment, I couldn't understand why. Here I was, little more than an out of work maid, being told I was actually some sort of princess. The part didn't fit. Deep down, I didn't feel good enough for that role. Ever since I had met my wife, I'd tried to make my life worthy of living. Every single day I had worked, really hard, to live up to how I saw her. She left early most days and I didn't want to be just one of those people who sat around a pool. I had invested my all into making our family great, our home clean, and myself worthy of her love and devotion. I paled in my own eyes in comparison to her.

I could look at this moment and see the imbalance. This house was in both our names, but in reality, it was Sarah's income who paid for it. The lights, the water, our food, the very clothes on my back were all paid for by her. She left each morning early to face the hardships of the cooperate world while I dabbled in cooking and decorating. I was so ashamed to ask for anything more.

She saw something in my face that made her stop. She stopped smiling and stopped the bath water, "What is it? I thought you'd be so happy with an entire day to yourself, with this new chapter. I mean, look around, Jess. We've *made* it!" Her voice was low, intense, full of love, and excitement.

How could I explain how undeserving of her love I was? Or how afraid I was of my dark future? Or how I hated my dependence on her? Tears streamed down my face and I just turned away. I couldn't talk.

"Maybe, you just are tired, I can let you rest tonight and I will make breakfast in the morning."

She turned the tap back on and helped me into the water. I drew up my knees, really sobbing now with no idea how to keep any of my feelings in anymore.

I wanted this life, *this* life we were living. I needed it. I didn't want it to change. I'd been doing too long to do anything else. I wanted to yell, to scream at time to stand still, save me from actually having to find myself. I was so much better at serving them. I didn't want to uncover old wounds or even heal my broken soul. I wanted to keep on pushing down all those pains and just serve my little family, was that too much to ask?

I didn't want to feel undeserving of her love. I didn't want my children to grow up. I didn't want to keep being the maid, but I felt there was nothing else I could do.

"Look, Jess, I know a lot is going on but I can't understand what is wrong. Can you tell me?"

I nodded, "I can try." I told her how afraid I was, how I didn't compare to her in anyway and finally, I told her I couldn't understand how someone like her could love someone like me.

When I finished spilling my soul to her, I opened my eyes and looked up. Her mouth was slightly open, her eyes filled with shocked sadness.

"All this time, all my hard work, I thought you knew. I thought you knew I was doing it for us, for you. How could you miss that, Jess? I thought you loved our home, our life. Where did I go wrong?"

I wasn't sure where it had gone wrong either. I did know I was afraid. I was so very afraid and I didn't know how to ask for help because right now, I was pretty sure I was not deserving of one more thing Sarah could provide.

She let me take my bath and I leaned back into the water thinking.

I tried to calm my thoughts and I felt like the crying had actually helped. I understood I was going through a depression, possibly even a mid-life crisis.

I wasn't sure where to go from this point, that was all. I understood, realized, was very aware the life I'd lived thus far might be too idealistic for most people in our world today. I'd tried to make myself worthy for all I'd been given in life. I was afraid because I could not see a future that needed me nor that I felt I deserved.

Over the next few days, I felt as if more and more of my role was unraveling. I still did the same things but it seemed as if everyone finally saw through my *façade* of importance; the three of them finally understood anyone could do the necessary chores and running around. The new awareness I'd gained of my own non-importance seemed to grow and I willingly withdrew.

A few weeks living like this, I noticed no one seemed to notice I was different. No one asked me how my days were. We were so busy one day kept turning into another and another. Finally, on a Thursday, Sarah called and asked me to go to a fancy dinner her office was having that very evening. She told me it was formal, black and white only.

I went to my closet and looked for something, anything that might hide my sagging body and heavy soul. I finally decided on a little black suit I'd owned forever; Sarah once told me was striking. I hung it in my doorway. The rest of the day I, of course, spent readying for Chloe and Jordan. I wanted them to have a good dinner and nice evening even if I was away. I scrubbed and cooked until it was time to get them.

As I drove to the school, I realized I was feeling anxious. Everything was making me anxious. The traffic, the noise, a song came on that I didn't like. I tried deep breathing but nothing seemed to calm my heart. I told myself I was fine and carried on. I greeted Chloe, then Jordan with false bravado, telling them I would be going out tonight. Sarah was getting honored at work. I told them how proud I was. They were happy for her and told me I would have a great time.

"What are you going to wear, Mom?" Chloe had always liked clothes. She must have gotten that from Sarah.

"Oh, just that little black suit. I know it's just my old go-to but I still like it."

I saw Chloe's eyes in the rear-view, her nose slightly wrinkled. I tried not to let that hurt.

"I wonder what mom is wearing," I heard her but I waited to respond. Sarah was being honored so she was out shopping. A few blocks later, she texted us a picture of a beautiful, sleek dress. It was knee length, still business professional but of course, Sarah made clothes look good. Not the other way around. I showed Chloe.

"Well, I think she got something for it. It's actually a big deal, she's being given an award for her work," I smiled at them.

"And you're just wearing that old suit? What did you do all day? You always have time for shopping, don't you?"

"Well, that is hurtful, Chloe. You know I am busy all day, too, I just decided I didn't need anything new. All eyes are on Sarah tonight, anyways."

I had to blink back some tears.

"So, what did you do all day?"

I didn't answer, and we drove the rest of the way listening to some horrible new band Jordan was into.

Later, I showered and dressed. I chose a beautiful yellow-gold necklace the kids had given me for the past Christmas. It really was the best one I owned and the color was perfect against the black. As I buttoned it, I noticed the fabric was slightly frayed. God, I hoped no one else would notice.

I kissed the kids goodbye and told them dinner was in the oven. I had done all their laundry, too, so I asked they ensure that was all picked up and I left the house. Sarah instructed me to hire a car; wine was being served. I settled into the back seat, relieved to be away from the house, but anxious to be on my way to an event where I didn't know anyone but my wife.

Sarah was always excited to have me go to such events. She performed them spectacularly. She always had a drink in her hand but never seemed to get intoxicated. No matter what she wore, she looked professional, stylish, and sexy. Her hair and minimalistic make-up were always perfect. She knew what to say to everyone and her smile gleamed the entire night. Only when we got into the car at the end would some of her performance wind down. Even then, she had the energy to make out on the way home, and carry on once we were in our own room.

I sighed. I was the opposite at the events. I had the drink, felt its effects in the first hour and my smile wasn't bright. Sarah introduced me proudly but when she walked away, I often got asked, "Sorry, so what exactly do you *do* all day?" I would then explain I raised the children while Sarah was working. It had been fine when the children were younger but now, I was often asked what I did since they were in school. I told myself to not bother, I had simply chosen a different life path but the thing was, it somehow *did* matter. And it seemed to matter more and more every day. I asked myself over and again, "Just what *have* I done for the past two decades?"

By the time I got to the event, I was feeling more than a little overwhelmed. I didn't see Sarah when I first entered, so I headed straight for the bar. It was cocktail hour, after all. I ordered my favorite, dirty, dirty martini, extra olives. I drank it straight down and ordered another. I felt a little calmer as I stepped away from the bar, looking for my wife.

It took nearly twenty minutes, but she finally came in, looking a little harried but gorgeous. She was so gorgeous I highly doubted anyone could notice the harried part. Her new dress was so perfect on her tiny waist, showing just enough of her beautiful skin off, fitted but not tight. I was so proud of her. I looped my arm around her waist and told her how beautiful she looked. She was absolutely radiant. I kissed her and she responded, kissing me back.

"Thanks for coming! I didn't realize I was getting the highest honor tonight, and you look great, too," she linked arms with me, "I want a drink, too, then I can introduce you to a few people."

Sarah was always so lovely to me, even if she was lying. I knew I didn't look great. My suit was the same age as Chloe and even though it was expensive, the style was dated. Maybe it was the alcohol but the frayed fabric seemed even more noticeable in this lighting. I hadn't done much to my hair or face either, so I knew I looked at least ten years older than Sarah, who was actually older than me by two years. I just smiled and let her lead back to the bar though. She ordered herself a drink and one more for me. I finished off my second and picked up the third.

We turned and surveyed the room, arms linked again. Sarah pointing out the various up and ups. We crossed the room and looked for our seats. *At least, I have her by my side*, I thought. It was a comfort to be with someone so sure of themselves, even in this situation. If she wasn't there or hadn't shown up for some reason, I think I would have left. The alcohol eased some but not all my anxiety, especially as I looked at the other guests.

Everyone looked as if they were wearing new clothes. They all looked as if they'd visited the salon that afternoon. No event I had ever been to had so many perfect looking people in one room. I tried not to comb my fingers through my hair.

"I have another surprise," Sarah told me softly as we eyed the tables for our names, "They invited the *Times!* Our project has gone so well, we will be a feature story." She was almost shaking, she was so excited.

"Wow! That is so amazing!" I lifted my glass to her and took a swallow. I hoped my words weren't too slurred. She smiled and drank a little, too.

"Oh, here we are! Head table!" and she pointed to an elegantly lettered *Sarah* right at the top, middle table. I looked to the right, then the left. I didn't see my name.

"Oh good, you found your place," a dapper looking man was kissing Sarah's right cheek, "And who is this?" He reached is hand towards me.

"Oh, Bob, this is my wife, Jess," Sarah introduced us.

"Aw, the power behind the woman, eh? We sure are proud to call Sarah one of our own, the work she does, the energy she brings just has made the world of difference to the company. What a lucky lady you are to call her wife."

"Bob, that is so generous!" I was surprised to see Sarah color a little. This guy must be really important.

"So nice to meet you, Bob," I said, "I certainly find myself lucky to have Sarah. She's been a wonderful provider for our family. Not to mention a fantastic mom." Sarah squeezed my hand and mouthed, "Thank you."

"Alright, well, I will see you ladies in a bit. I'm seated here, too, but I am going help myself at that bar. Would you care for another?"

Both Sarah and I nodded. I was still looking for my name card.

"Oh, only honorees are at this table. Their guests are seated towards the back," Bob pointed, "We thought that might be a better view for you guys because the cameras will all be lined up here." He smiled warmly and walked away.

My heart beat a little faster. I was going to have to go sit with the trophy wives. I hadn't prepared myself for such evening. I tried to hide how disappointed I was and smiled a little at Sarah, who I was relieved to see was looking disappointed.

"No big deal, babe. After all, this is to honor all the hard work and dedication you have given. It really is your night."

My words were a little sloppy but I hoped dinner and water would help. I smiled at her again.

"Well, I didn't know that is how they were doing things, are you sure you'll be alright?"

I smiled and even managed a little laugh, "I am a grown-up. I know where I belong."

I winked at her and she kissed my cheek.

"Linda! Hi! I guess we are all seated here and they have our guests over there," Sarah was greeting another co-worker, "They say it will be best, so everyone can see better."

"Oh, you brought someone? I didn't even ask my husband, I didn't think most liked this scene; unless it was about them. You know how men are," Linda's voice was hoarse, deeper than you expect seeing her petite frame.

"Well, yes, I brought my wife," Sarah pointed to me, "Jess, Linda, Linda, Jess."

"Oh. I guess we haven't met before, pleasure."

Her hand was cold and I had to force my smile. She didn't return it.

"Well, I am going to go sit, it looks as if most people are settling in. Good luck!" I kissed Sarah and turned to find my own table. I was seated with my back towards the stage and there were only two other guests at the table across from me. They didn't say much as I sat. Bob placed a fresh drink as I sat and hurried to his own seat.

I turned around as best as I could but my seat of awful. Even with us placed in the back, the cameras blocked most of the view and the microphone went out again and again. I couldn't see and I couldn't hear. At least, they were bringing the food out soon and I could get something in me besides all that alcohol.

Our table was last to be served and when they finally got around to us, we were informed all that was left was the vegetarian meal. I normally like vegetarian just fine, but I'd had all those drinks and needed that protein. I sighed and accepted my food.

Now the formalities were over, the other two at the table tried making small talk but they knew each other already and had their own inside jokes. Both were typical long, blond haired women with perfect make-up. They each obviously came from money. I didn't have much to say.

I saw one glance at my plain nails, a look of small disgust on her face. "So, who are you here with?" one finally asked me.

I told her my wife was Sarah, the main honoree. She glanced at the other one.

"Oh, okay, I see now," and not another word from either of them was directed towards me. I smiled and excused myself. I walked to the bar and stayed.

I must have sat for a good thirty minutes when I decided I needed to use the restroom. By then, I'd had another drink but somehow found my way. Then, the shit really hit the fan.

I opened the door and practically fell into a crowded room with a line. Thankfully, most women were touching up their faces, it seemed. I saw the two I had eaten with and waved at them. They looked a little mortified but I guess in my drunken state I didn't notice. Or maybe I just didn't care. I had seen one hand;

the other, a pill from a small bottle in her purse. I had never done so much as smoke weed before.

"I'd like some, please," I had no idea what those pills were, but I wanted out of feeling. I was done, even in my drunken state, I knew I was done. I held out my hand. To my surprise, she handed me the bottle. Maybe she just wanted to get away from me or maybe I was being louder than I thought, whatever her reason, she just handed it right over. I lowered it over my open mouth and took the entire contents all in one go. I don't recall anything else from that night.

Two days later, I woke in a brightly lit hospital room.

I was on my own and the curtains were opened. I had no idea what time it was or what hospital was my current home. I had an I.V. and my head felt as if I were under water. I felt dirty. I reached up to feel my hair, it was a little matted. I stretched my legs and noticed my left knee hurt at the slightest movement or touch.

Carefully, I rolled to one side and looked for my phone. It was plugged in, lying on a small bedside table. I picked it up. Numerous missed calls and several missed texts were blinking back at me. The time was 2:24. Judging there was sun out, I decided it must be just after two p.m. I rolled back to my back and tried to recall how I had landed, here, in the hospital.

At first, I couldn't recall anything from the entire day from Sarah's promotion. There were a few moments I panicked a little, wondering if I had been in some sort of accident.

With a lot of effort, I remembered my suit, seeing the frayed edge on the jacket. Then my memory flashed to my wife. I smiled a little thinking of how beautiful Sarah was that night. Then I remembered the martinis. I pictured the awful women who shared the same table. Finally, I remembered going back to the bar for another drink. I couldn't recall anything else. I...I closed my eyes, feeling shame fill me up.

I wondered how inebriated I had gotten to land me here in this hospital. How embarrassing for Sarah and on her special night. Tears came into my eyes. I was so selfish. I wondered what else happened.

Plus! How were my kids? Who had brought them to school that morning? Tears fell in earnest then and I felt so alone. I had screwed up my one gig. I wondered how Sarah and my children could ever forgive me.

"Oh, you're awake, good," a kind, determined voice sounded from the door, "You hungry?"

I shook my head, my hands in my hair, "I want to go home." My words were an ashamed whisper.

"Well, you will have to ask the doc about that," she crossed the room and looked down at me.

"I'd like to call my family, please."

"You don't know what has happened, do you?" her voice wasn't exactly unkind but it wasn't overly warm either, "You have been here nearly two whole days. I wasn't too sure you'd be okay, when or if you woke up. You want to talk about anything?"

Two days! Two? My mind echoed her words and I just shook my head. I couldn't look into her eyes.

"I can call your wife, the one who admitted you. She told me if you wake up, tell you not to worry, you can talk later. The kids are fine," she was taking my vitals and I still couldn't look her in the eyes.

She tried telling me I needed to eat something, tried getting me to talk a little more, but I wasn't hungry and I wasn't ready to talk. She finally squeezed my shoulder a little and lifted my trembling chin.

"Look, I don't know why you did what you did. I never do know why people do what they do. I do know you are safe though, you have been given another chance. I know you are loved by that special woman who has called every hour on the hour since she admitted you. I also know you can do better."

With those words, she left my room.

I lay a little while longer in the bed, crying until I fell asleep. The next time I woke, Sarah was standing by my side, smoothing my hair away from my face. Her eyes were full of tears.

"Hey there," she said softly, picking up my hand, and kissing it. I couldn't speak. Tears just ran down my tired face. She leaned onto the bed, holding me, rocking back and forth. Our shoulders shook and shook. "I thought I'd lost you," she finally whispered.

Funny, I thought I'd lost her. Here she was though and it looked like I was going to be alright. I needed to beg her forgiveness but the words caught in my throat. I wasn't sure if the three people I loved most could or would forgive me. The thought actually made me sick to my stomach and had I eaten anything before, I would have lost it right then.

Sarah leaned me back onto my pillows, "When they found you in the bathroom, you were hardly breathing. Your lips were blue. Someone told me they thought you had some drinks and took some sort of pill, is that true?" Her voice was gentle and I nodded. I couldn't remember exactly, but her words sounded true.

"Do you normally take pills?"

I shook my head, "No, that was a first," my words were whispered.

"Well, someone called an ambulance and they cleared your tummy right there."

That might have been why my throat was sore, I realized.

"Then they got you hooked up to this I.V. right away and brought you here. Someone said you had told them you were so happy to be "done." Her voice was still so gentle and hearing the events from that night, I knew they were true. I hadn't realized I'd said anything about being done, not out loud, at least.

I looked down at my hands. I couldn't look into her eyes any more than I'd been able to with the nurse.

"Do you feel like that today?"

I made myself look into her wide, intelligent eyes. They were full of tears. Then, I looked towards the window. I didn't know how I felt. I felt bad, so bad for making her worry.

"What did you tell the kids?"

She looked at me so sadly, "I told them what I knew, and that was that you had a lot to drink and someone gave you pills. Jordan said he thought you had looked sad before you left. And Chloe said she thought you had been looking sad for a while."

"Do they hate me?"

My hands were shaking with fear and my fingertips felt so cold.

"Jess, no one hates you. How could we? You're our everything," she hugged me again and I felt so safe in her arms, "I just want to get to the bottom of this and get you what you need, okay?"

She sat down, crossed legged on a small part of the bed. It felt so good to have her so near me. I finally told her how I had been feeling for far too long. She never got upset, just held my hand and listened. When I told her about the suit, she suggested getting a new one.

"For what? What is the point?" I didn't need new clothes, they weren't going to get me better, I certainly didn't need to dress up for work or anything. She didn't argue, just rubbed my forearm.

"They are going to release you tomorrow afternoon. You will have to talk with a doctor either this evening or in the morning, okay? I can help you shower if you would like."

And after all I had put her through, my wife helped me shower and dress in soft pajamas she'd so thoughtfully packed. She didn't ask me more questions and even though I thought and thought, I couldn't figure out what really happened that night.

I didn't understand how *I* had gotten to this point. Even in my youth, I'd never gotten so drunk like that. I had standards. I was proving to the world and myself that two mothers could raise as good a family as any. I'd worked hard to make our home nice, give the kids everything they deserved. Yet, here I was recovering from an *episode* in the hospital! I felt lower than low. I had failed at all of it and I wasn't so sure there would be another chance on any of this.

After years of struggling with my own self-worth, I don't believe I ever felt so low as after my attempt to end my own life.

Sarah's kindness only exacerbated my anxiety, adding to my belief I had done nothing with my precious gift of life and the really exquisite way I lived. I really felt I had done nothing to deserve Sarah's love or my children's love. Any good thing I did, I minimized because I believed most of what I did was so menial.

I couldn't hold back those thoughts or feelings any more. I tried but the doctor saw right through me. I was diagnosed with severe depression and prescribed twice weekly sessions with a professional. I was also, thankfully, given anti-anxiety meds that I could take up to four times a day. I numbly made my next appointments but Sarah was the one who put them in both mine and her phones. Then, I was discharged.

I was dressed and clean but honestly, I looked more than awful. I hadn't bothered doing my hair, not even blowing it dry with the hair dryer. It just hung to my head. Sarah brought jeans and sweats for me to wear but I hadn't even put on the jeans. I wore gray sweats that were too big and a long-knit sweater for the journey home. I liked how warm it was, how it covered me up so well. Sarah drove while I looked out the window remembering nothing we passed. She stopped for a cup of coffee before we made it home.

I followed her inside and allowed her to order for me. She was struggling, I could tell, with how down I was. God help me, I was trying. I just felt so empty. I hadn't answered any of her questions or responded to most of what she had said. I had asked about the kids, of course, but even that drained what little energy I had.

Now I was going to face the horrible things I had done, own up to them to my own children. I couldn't see how they could ever forgive me.

"Look at me, Jess," Sarah was saying, "I have talked to the kids about this and I have told them everything I know about depression and anxiety. You can do this. You feel bad, I can tell. We love you, though. We love you so much."

Her normally confident voice had taken on a pleading tone. She took my hand.

I could feel tears sliding down my cheeks I hadn't even realized were formed in my eyes.

"I don't know what to tell them," I heard myself whisper.

I had thought of little else during my stay in the hospital. I couldn't think what to tell my children about my suicide attempt or why I felt the way I did. *How could I?* echoed again and again through my mind.

"I have told them everything there is to be said about depression. I think all they need, all they want is to hug you. You don't have to say anything."

There, again, I was being loved more than I could ever deserve, more than I could ever earn, or more than I could ever pay back. I shook my head. I wasn't deserving of such love. My throat hurt again.

She finished her coffee and led me back to the car. Not even ten minutes later, we pulled into the drive in front of our house. The kids were on the doorstep waiting.

Jordan was standing, tall and silent, his arms folded in front of his chest. Chloe was sitting, her knees drawn up to her chest. When we pulled in, neither moved. Sarah rushed around and opened my door.

"We can do this together," she whispered and took my hand. She led me up the path to our home.

As we neared, both the kids were standing, arms to their sides. Chloe reached for me first and put her face in my hair, crying. Jordan took me in his arms and pulled both of us to him. Sarah wrapped her arms around all of us, best as she could, and we stood in front of our house holding each other for longer than I could ever remember doing.

I felt so safe.

I followed Chloe inside. We all ended up in the kitchen and Sarah put on some tea. Jordan and Chloe sat close to me at the table holding my hands. I was having a hard time looking into their eyes. No one spoke.

I didn't know what to say. I was sorry but not because I had tried it. I was sorrier it hadn't worked and now, I felt I was more of a burden than ever to my precious family. How does someone apologize for that?

"I love you, Mommy," Chloe whispered.

"I love you too, Mom, so much," Jordan's voice was so hoarse it startled me and I looked up. Both were silently crying.

I was shocked. No one was angry. They just wanted me there. And even though I couldn't understand why they felt I was worth having around or how I was going to fix myself, I vowed I would.

8

For the next few days, maybe even weeks, my brain was so foggy, I can't recall exactly, I forced myself out of bed each day and dressed. I took the kids to school and tried to keep up on the house. I noticed Sarah called a lot more. She sent texts throughout the day. It was so nice. I tried not to dwell on the reasons why.

I went to all my appointments and really tried to find the help I knew I needed. It was much more difficult than I ever could have imagined. I had made a vow though and I aimed to keep it.

My first therapist was awful. She was older than me by about fifteen years. I believe she had been in some sort of accident because she kept shifting her weight from leg to leg and she frequently got up to limp around her office. After talking for less than ten minutes, I found I didn't really care for her. I felt she must be doing this simply because she needed a paycheck. She asked me why I was there at precisely the exact time I was wondering the same about her.

I pointed out my file had been sent over by the hospital when they had discharged me for attempted suicide. She raised her eyebrows and sat down across from me. She sighed. At that point, I really thought she was going to have some sort of advice for me. I expected her to challenge me to rise up, be stronger. I was wrong.

"Life is weird, you know? It's all ups and downs and let me tell you, no matter what age you are, that never changes. Hell, it might even get worse. I read your file and I saw how much you drank that night. That is a lotta juice. Why did you do that? Do you do that often, how often do you drink?"

Her tone was accusatory.

She went on, "You know, I have some years on you and I have always had to work. I don't know what you have done to add your worth to this world, but I have always had to work earning my own way. When I thought I had finally made it, I get hit by a truck in some parking lot. It happened just up the street from here. This last year, I've endured three surgeries and I still have pain in my leg. Its things like getting hit by a truck that really put life into perspective. I could have died. But I fought back and here I am at work. I dress the part, I am respectable."

She glanced at my sweats.

"I don't know what pushed you, but I can tell you I am so sick of seeing able people drink away their lives. I just can't understand and what's more, I won't. So, I am going to tell you what I think is best for you, join A.A. Do the twelve steps and stop letting your family down."

And with that, she stopped talking to me and pulled out her phone. I had been there for less than twenty minutes. I was stunned into silence.

I sat for a moment, not knowing what to do, but she never looked at me again. I could feel the tears on my face as I gathered my things and stood to leave. They were really falling as I pushed open the door. She never said another word.

Sarah called a little while later to ask how it went. I didn't know where to start. I told her I needed to find someone else.

Looking back, I have no idea why I was treated that way in that appointment. I hadn't been able to explain myself at all, nor even given the chance to answer the couple of questions she fired away at me. Shame and guilt absolutely overwhelmed me as I somehow drove myself home. I wasn't even sure how I made it home. As I parked the car, I felt my resolve deepen. I had to find another way; I couldn't survive another appointment like that.

The next appointment was a much better experience. I found it on my own and upon my first entrance, I knew I was in the right place. It was too colorful. Too cheerful. Instead of plain, professionally subtle colors and decorations, hues of every shade blasted from everywhere. I wasn't sure what Sarah would think of the therapist or the office; both were a bit odd.

The therapist was a very short, very old, Japanese-American woman. Her office was cluttered and she was twenty minutes late. I counted three cats while I was waiting and three more when she invited me to sit. She was as colorful as her office. Her shirt was red. Her pants blue. Her shoes were orange flats. She wore purple glasses. I tried not to stare.

She stared at me, though, unashamedly. She looked at me and took a deep breath. She really studied me for a good ten minutes before speaking while I tried not to fidget. Finally, "You are a full-time mother?" was uttered, her voice was soft.

I nodded.

"And your children are teens now?" Again, I nodded. She smiled, "I am surprised I haven't seen you before. That is not a life for the faint of heart. Tell me all about your family."

I was shocked. I felt my mouth open but no sound came out. I had not expected that. It took a few moments to compose myself.

"Well, I have been married about sixteen years. My wife's name is Sarah, you'd like her. She's perfect. She is a little taller than me. A lot thinner. She's nice and smart. She's funny."

"You had the babies, then?"

I nodded, wondering how she knew that, "Yes, well anyways, Sarah is fit, perfect hair. You know the type. She has worked really hard to be where she is. She even herself through school by joining the military. We met when she got out. Now she works at a posh place in the city doing something for the environment. When we met, I couldn't figure out why she even looked my way twice. I'd just gotten out of college and was working in an arts store. I loved it. I loved working there."

I closed my eyes briefly at the memory of my first real job.

"The people were all great and I taught a lot. I taught crafting and art therapy. It didn't do anything for the world, not like Sarah's job, but I liked being around happy people, doing happy things. After Sarah proposed, we decided we needed more income so I quit there and wrote for a local paper. It was a good job but not as much fun as working at that arts store."

The memories of our early days poured from me. It felt good, recalling how I once felt, how I'd planned life with my fiancée.

"I told her early on how I dreamt of becoming a mother. She was so excited for us. And when she proposed, she told me she felt like she was really building a life. Like it was the most real thing she had ever done. Our wedding was small, intimate, and very happy. We both wore white dresses. Mine was lace-covered, hers was plainer but more glamorous. We were so happy. A few years later, we had the perfect baby boy. We named him Jordan. "He was all boy," I laughed, "Quite the surprise, as you can imagine! We weren't sure what we had signed up for and by the time he was only three, we welcomed a sweet girl we called Chloe. Jordan is a soccer player, he's already been talking scholarships. Chloe loves to read and swim." I felt warm, just talking about our family, the life we'd built.

The therapist smiled.

"My wife has done really well. We live in a lovely home and we have plenty to live on. In fact, Sarah just announced a couple months ago, she can retire in a year. And that's the thing," I swallowed hard, keeping the tears back as best as I could. "I know I shouldn't complain. I shouldn't feel any pain. After all, I have so much. My children are smart, healthy, each at the top of their classes. I have the love of my life beside me."

I tried to take a deep breath and hiccupped a little.

"But every time I think of *me,* I can't help but feel inadequate. I haven't done anything to deserve any of this. I haven't worked in almost two decades. I haven't contributed to our savings. I certainly don't have a retirement to add to our salary when that time comes. Everything I do, I know anyone else can do. In fact, most anyone else could probably do a better job. I can't even look in the mirror anymore. My wife is fit and beautiful. Then, there's me. I have the sagging tummy. The sagging boobs. I hate my body. Even though the kids are in school all day, I don't find the time to make it to the gym. I dress like an old mom. Every day I find myself hoping my kids will take after my wife. Worse, I can see they do, too. Who would want to end up as me? I depend on everyone for my very existence." That truth hurt more than a little, a stab right through my heart. I'd worked so hard for our family. I sacrificed so much and no one wanted to be me when they grew up. I felt cold and started shivering.

She watched me for a few moments. She handed me brightly colored tissue box. She said nothing while I wiped my nose, then my eyes.

Finally, "Tell me, what is your favorite color?"

"What? Oh, I don't know. I decorated our house in mostly grays because Sarah likes that so much. She says too much color makes her feel tired."

I looked around the office a little guiltily.

"I like grays, too, I really do, but I guess I was a little more colorful at one point."

I waved my arm indicating the room's colors.

She nodded, "You know when we are small if you remember yourself or your children, one of the first thing we identify as "ours" is our favorite color. What is your favorite hobby?"

I looked at her. I had just opened up to this woman and she was making weird small talk? My face showed my disappointment, I could feel it.

Sighing, I said, "I don't know. I guess I like keeping the house clean, you know, taking care of them. Or at least that's what I do most of the time. I don't want to just free-load off Sarah." I looked down at my hands. Truthfully, I didn't know what my favorite hobby was or what I did with free time. I hadn't let myself have free time in a long time.

"You know, Jess, I don't know if you know anything about mid-life but it sneaks up on us. Its fast and most of the time, we didn't even notice it lurking, ready to get us when we least expect it. We build lives with and for everyone we love. After all, that is what it takes, isn't it?

It takes a lot of time and work and sacrifice," she nodded quietly, "And then, *boom*!" She clapped her hands making me jump. She laughed a little, "And before you know it, you are staring at mid-life right between the eyes and is daring you to take a step away from the safety of the life you built. Do you understand?"

My heart was still pounding. I licked my lips and watched her for a moment.

"So, I'm lost? Or maybe I lost myself a little?"

She nodded, "Yes, I think so."

I wasn't so surprised, I realized once it was said out loud. After all, I couldn't even answer small talk questions. I hadn't done much for myself for a long time. I guess I forgot somethings. That awareness made me feel a little better, a little lighter than I had in a very long time.

"So, yes, you are lost. What do lost people do?" she asked.

I tried to think. I guess most people tried to figure out where they were, so I said that.

"Very good. Yes. You are trying to figure out where you are right now. Can you answer that?" she asked.

I sat and thought. I finally decided no, I couldn't figure out where I was.

I shook my head *no*.

I'd started this life with a dream of motherhood and living with my best friend. I dreamed of having a house we both might love. Why was I so unfulfilled if I had my dreams? The therapist gave me time to think.

I sat and thought of all I had done. *The therapist was absolutely right,* I thought her "Boom!" echoed through my mind. Mid-life had snuck up on me. I had been building and building but with no real plans for a finished product.

I felt like I was standing at the top of a magnificent unfinished building. All I'd accomplished was way down at the first floors; so far away and no way to go back. There was nothing at the top. I tried to really visualize what I felt like, what that image made me feel.

I told her, "I guess I feel as if I am at the top of a finished stair case that doesn't lead anywhere. Except I can't go back either. It's like that part is blocked. I can't go forward either though, because I'll fall."

"Excellent, excellent. Okay. So. There you are on your staircase and I guess you have run out of room or maybe materials that you were using. At least, we now know where to start. I will see you next time, not so early, okay?" She nodded at her own words.

I nodded back and made the next appointment. As I left, I felt lighter but I couldn't explain just why. I felt good but wondered how. I didn't feel as if I'd made some earth-shattering self-discovery but I still felt better.

I tried not to think about it too much.

Once I got home, I sat on the couch. I decided to order dinner in and put that in before I had to go get the kids. I was smiling when I picked them up.

On the drive, I asked each how their days were and what their plans were for the night. I reminded Jordan we needed to practice driving this weekend, he was due for his test next month. I saw him and Chloe exchange a look but I ignored it and dropped them off at their practices with hugs.

Normally, I would just go in to sit and wait, but it was a nice day, so I stayed outside a little while longer. At first, I just rolled my window down and enjoyed the cool spring air. Then I got out and walked up one side of the street and down the next. The fresh air felt glorious, invigorating. I used to love outdoor walks.

Dinner and Sarah were waiting when we got home. We talked and laughed around the table for a long time. I fell asleep in Sarah's arms on the couch, just like when we first moved in together. The next day was good, too.

Sarah made us coffee and even went into work a little later than normal. We dropped the kids off together and went for a quick walk. She finally left, waving happily all the way down the street. I smiled and waved back, then turned back to our home.

All day, I did what I always did. I cleaned and prepared for the evening ahead, the next day and the following days. The rest of the week followed in pretty much the same way. By Sunday evening, I was exhausted, even after a weekend of mostly relaxing.

Monday morning, I noticed my mind was in overdrive again. I reminded myself of how great the last few days had been but, I could feel myself slipping. I drove to the appointment, full of apprehension.

How could I tell the therapist how I was doing today? I had worked so hard, only to be in almost the exact same state as the week before. I hoped she wouldn't think I wasn't working on this.

"So, how was your week?" she started before I even sat down. I burst into tears. She waited a little while, handed me the bright tissue box, allowing the tears to dry a little, "Let me guess, you felt great after leaving here last week, then you went home, and had a wonderful evening. Maybe even the next day or two were almost perfect. You even told yourself, 'Things are back to normal.' But then, you felt yourself getting down. Was there any one thing that triggered this?"

"How did you know all that? How could you possibly have known all that about my week?" I was astounded. I was too surprised to even answer her question.

She smiled, "I have been a therapist for a long time. People come here, they talk, they discover, and they leave feeling much better. The thing is, though, healing from depression is not the same as healing from a flu. It would be nice, but it is not the same. Depression is not something that just leaves the body like a germ or virus does. As you discover yourself more, you will discover your triggers, you will learn to be completely honest with yourself. Dealing with depression is as if you are a bow and arrow. You will get pulled backwards, perhaps many times, before going ahead. Even then, you might miss the target and get pulled back again. The trick is to keep trying."

Her words, the analogy made sense. I had experienced bouts of happiness and depression my entire life. Picturing a bow and arrow calmed me and I thought about her question.

I closed my eyes and said, "I don't think anything really triggered me. I took a few walks, I had the best time with my wife and kids. I just couldn't keep up the momentum." A few tears leaked out at my last words. I whispered, "Maybe I am just too weak?" My heart almost stopped, this thought scared me more than anything.

If I was too weak to tackle this now, would I ever be strong? If I couldn't beat this, how would I beat other obstacles life would continue to throw our way? After all, just because someone is ill, even physically, doesn't mean life gives anyone a break. I felt my breath quicken.

"You are taking an awful lot of responsibility for this. Has anyone told you that before?"

I thought about that.

I nodded at her, "I guess I understand depression is an illness but it seems like since it is in my mind, I should be able to will it out of me. After all, it doesn't need an operation like cancer or something. It feels like I should be able to control this." Again, my heart dropped at the words I was saying. I did not *feel* strong enough to will this out of me. The more I thought about it, the worse it made me feel. I pictured my life.

I lived an almost dream life. I had a beautiful home. My children were almost perfect. They were beautiful, able, and whole. My wife was amazing, beautiful, and hardworking. We had money, plenty of food, plenty of everything. I felt as if I was inviting bad karma by not continually being grateful for all I had. It made me miserable.

"Well, you are right, we cannot cut depression from our lives. I think it must reside somewhere between the physical and metaphysical plane. I wish we could cut it out, perhaps that would be easier. The truth is depression haunts many. Like any other illness, it can strike anyone, anytime. And unlike physical illnesses, it takes practice and acceptance to endure. Healing is different here."

Her voice was as calming as the words she spoke but my panic refused to be moved.

"What practice?" I demanded, "I am so tired already, I am exhausted of trying to fight this depression." A few more hot tears rolled down my cheeks that I didn't bother to wipe away.

"Well, that is part of the issue, you are fighting. It is exhausting to fight an invisible enemy the whole day through. How about you try not fighting. I want you take a deep breath." I breathed in. "No, deeper, like this!" she demanded me watch and imitate. I saw her chest fill and then beneath her rib cage expand.

"You breathe like you are a star opera singer. It takes practice. You have to exercise that diaphragm muscle. Try again."

So, there I sat, at nearly fifty years old, learning to breathe properly. I counted in my breath for five, held for five, and released through my nose for six. It was harder than it sounds and we practiced it for nearly ten minutes. I felt light-headed and closed my eyes, leaning my head on the back of her couch.

She said, "You need to breathe. Breathe in, accepting you have something you don't like in your life. Breathe that in, hold it. Now, as you breathe out, allow yourself to let it go. You do not need to fear it any longer. After all, you just accepted it. Have you ever tried hypnosis?"

I shook my head *no*. I no longer felt light headed, so I sat up straighter. I wasn't panicky anymore. I gave her my full attention.

She told me, "Hypnosis is simply finding a deeper awareness. Some people, throughout history, have told it is mind control but it is actually *you* relaxing into a state of awareness to understand more about yourself. I think we should try this, because you have some negative things to say and think about yourself. If you can remember why you think this way, you can change it. Finding this awareness and a new way to believe is much faster than normal talk therapy. Would you like to try this?"

She waited ever so patient while I thought about trying hypnotherapy for the first time.

I couldn't shake the fact I was skeptical. What she said made sense but I still had my doubts. I wondered what Sarah would think or say. I took another deep breath. Even though I was definitely skeptical, I couldn't think of one reason I shouldn't try it. After all, the worse that would happen is it would not work. I felt myself nodding.

"Okay, yes, I think I would like to try this. I wanted to get better before Sarah retires. I have less than a year now, only ten months or so now," my voice cracked a little. Only ten months to go! Thankfully, the deep breathing really had helped me feel less anxious. I could concentrate on her words and what they meant, even realizing Sarah's retirement loomed closer and even through my doubt. Self-awareness seemed like a good thing.

I knew I had neglected myself into this state. I constantly put everyone else's needs and wants before mine. I became so used to it, I didn't even question doing it anymore. I knew that had to change and I knew how difficult that change would be. I knew my kids were all but grown, they didn't need that level of care anymore. I knew Sarah was fine, more than fine. She had done so much without needing that sort of sacrifice from me for a long time. I don't know if she even understood or realized the sacrifices, I had made for the three of them. I never told her, never explained it. I hadn't thought I would ever need to. I was comfortable with sacrifice though. For years, I thought all of it was worth it; I had talked myself into believing it was all worth it, that it was all necessary. It was time to find out why I thought that and more importantly, how to change it.

The therapist indicated I should lie back and get comfortable, "All I am going to do is act as your guide. You will always be in control, deep breath, I can see you are nervous. You are only going to get very relaxed in your mind, so you can think without interruption. We have two parts that control our lives. The first is our subconscious. That is what you need to understand, what lies in your subconscious; that is why we use hypnosis. Our other part, the conscience, is what we use most of the time to get us through our daily routines, solve problems and that sort of thing. It is driven by the subconscious. Think of a big clock, all the gears that drive each other. We act according to what our subconscious knows, even though we may not have to think about it. We just do it. If you can understand why you talk so harshly to yourself, where that began, you can also teach yourself a new, healthy way to talk to yourself. Any questions? Good, I want you to lie back then, and get very comfortable. Keep your arms and legs uncrossed, yes, cover yourself with that blanket. Good idea and I want you to count back from ten. Deep breath in and ten, nine, eight, deep breath in, and hold it. Seven, release, six, five, deep breath in, and hold it. Four, release, and deep breath in, three, hold it. Hold it. Two, one, release."

I followed her soft words to the letter. I could feel my heart slow, my breathing slowed, and I stopped worrying in less than five minutes, just listening to her words. She spoke with intention, slowly and unhurriedly, assuring me we were in this together and continued to guide my breathing.

"I want you to envision yourself standing at a large door. In just a moment, we are going to go through that door, not yet, we have time. Just breathe. I think you will notice thoughts might come but allow them to leave. You are in control. You do not have to linger on any thoughts. I want you to think about that door. Stand in front of it, put your palm on it. Your childhood is on the other side. In just a moment, you will visit it, and see and understand why you think the way you do. You are going to understand your childhood from your adult perspective. Nothing behind that door can harm you, it is just a memory after all. I want you to see, but not connect to what you see. You are not experiencing anything again, you are just watching. Go ahead, open the door."

I pushed open that door with all my might. It was a giant of a door; taller and wider than most. It was heavy and wooden. At this point, I could hear my therapist, but her voice was no longer my focus. I had walked through that door, right up to the house we lived in as I grew up.

It wasn't a large house, nor on the best street but it had been home. It was small and white. It was old, older than the houses around it. The yard was neat as a pin, thanks to the close attentions from my mother. The yard and house were always in perfect order. Always. I looked up at the door. I decided to go inside.

It was just as I recalled. The smell of her favorite cleaner was mixed with baking cookies. I walked through the living room and looked into the kitchen. It was spotless. My own home, my adult home, was clean, but this was pristine. I didn't lean on the walls or the doorways, I didn't want to leave fingerprints. My own home was painted with a shiny, slightly gray color, so you can't see any handprints. In this home, they were simply non-existent even on the matte, white walls due her constant reminders not to touch the walls. There were no dishes on the counter, nor in the sink. In fact, there was no dust on the cabinet fronts, windowsills, light fixtures, or ceiling fans. The air vents were all smooth and dust-free, too. It was quiet, even though it was the middle of the day and there were people home.

I walked through the kitchen, back to the stairs that led up. My room was up there. I passed my sister's room. She was in there, playing with her dolls. She had the friend with red hair and they were quietly laughing. It was a picture-perfect moment that made me smile.

I kept walking slowly. I didn't need to hurry. My room door was closed. I paused in front of it, I wasn't sure I really wanted to go open that door. I thought about it, my therapist stayed silent. Finally, I took a deep breath in though and slowly pushed open the door.

At first, I couldn't see much. It took a little while to see the room that had once been adorned in the several green shades chosen by my mother. I remember her replacing some of my furniture one year for Christmas. I had only been about five, but she explained I was pretty grown up and instead of toys or dolls, I had gotten shelves and a dresser. They were there. My bed was covered in the rather scratchy bedspread I'd been given for my birthday the same year as the furniture. I'd never liked it. Not only was it scratchy but it was an ugly shade of green, trimmed in garish pink flowers. Time hadn't changed those particular feelings. I looked around a little more. Slowly, the rest of the room came into focus.

I was there, towards the back of the room and my mother stood before me. Her back was to me and her face bent very near towards the child in front of her. I knew what was happening.

It was late on a Friday afternoon. Every Friday, we were supposed to clean our rooms. We changed the sheets and dusted and vacuumed. I was seven. I hadn't cleaned to her standards and she was giving me a telling off. She was pointing to a shelf full of dolls. They were the kind with the porcelain faces. Each week though, I carefully cleaned the glass portion of them but their dresses grew dusty. I closed my eyes, but I could hear her angry, disappointed voice.

"What do you mean you didn't know you could vacuum their dresses, why wouldn't you know that? What else is this little attachment for?" I watched as she grabbed the child's face hard, "Look at me, now look at those, what is wrong with you, can't you even clean six simple dolls? You can do them again with the attachment. Use your head, Jess! What else would that attachment even be used for? You know what? I went in the bathroom just now. I saw the bath tub, you can do that again, too."

She turned and walked out of the room.

I looked at the child that had once been me. There I was, messy hair, it never was full enough or curly enough to be pretty. It was still messy. There weren't tears, even though I remembered how much her strong hands hurt my face. There was a quiet determination set on that little jaw.

I knew what she was thinking. She, I loved her, my mother, all she, I, wanted to do was help around the house. I saw her eyes change as a resolve set in; could see her resolve to do better, do more, stay out of the way more.

That resolve had lasted my lifetime as I tried to accommodate everyone else apologizing for taking up space, I never allowed for myself.

"Look, look at that child before you. Is that any way you treat your children?" a voice gently broke into the room.

I looked at the child. No, I couldn't say that was any way to treat a child. Even if her hair was messy. Even if she hadn't known how to properly dust off doll's dresses. Even if she was in the way. That was no way to treat a child.

"Tell her then, go on, take her in your arms, and tell her as much. Tell her what you understand, now that you are grown."

I scooped up that child, surprised she was so light, I had always been told I was chubby. I sat her on my lap on the low bed. And I looked into her eyes.

"Look, I know this is hard right now. And we never did figure out why she was so harsh. But it's not your fault. You didn't make her this way. You didn't make any of her days bad. I don't think she knew what to really do with children but this isn't right. And even though this hurt and you feel like you aren't worth much, you are.

And you will grow up. You will do better than all this." Tears were rolling down those little cheeks. I could feel how much this little girl needed these words right now, how much she wanted to believe them, even though it was very difficult. She nodded just a little.

"I can take you away from here, you don't have to stay here anymore. Not if you don't want to."

And I picked her up and took her out of that room, down the hall, out the pristine kitchen, and out the door. I put her gently down and took her hand. And we walked towards the door.

I was crying when my therapist called me into the present. She allowed me time and gave me space to feel. She silently gave me some tissues and took my hand.

"Would you like some water?" She was so kind.

I shook my head *no*. I didn't need any water. I tried to make sense of the memory I'd allowed myself to view after all these years.

I'd lost my mother a few years ago. I still missed her but our relationship had always been difficult. I'd always thought it had been me. I'd always been a messy child or so I had thought. I thought I made a lot of extra work for her and that I should have done more for her. This memory proved my long-held beliefs wrong.

The house was pristine and quiet. That day I had been in my own room, away from her, giving her the space she'd always wanted. My old room was cleaner than my room in my own grown up house. The dolls' dresses *were* dusty but my God, I was so little. The vacuum was as large as me! It had been such a chore, such a challenge, to use that thing.

The truth was, that Friday, she had been so mean to an innocent child who wanted nothing more than to help. That memory and others caused me to deny myself life. I denied myself until I nearly killed myself.

"Why?" I whispered as more tears streaked down my cheeks.

The therapist shook her head, "I don't know why or how people can treat children so cruelly. They do though. It happens a lot."

I nodded, my arms wrapped around my chest.

"It is time to make the next appointment. I think after this, I need to see you in two days, not a whole week." Again, I just nodded and stood. I gathered my things and left without another word.

Thankfully, I walked into a sunny day. I felt good, despite the profound sadness of that memory.

I hadn't thought too much of my childhood for a long time. Sure I had consciously raised my own children very differently, but I had told myself I was simply part of a new generation. We just did things differently. I remembered my dad telling us, one day, how good we had it. We had plenty to eat, a nice home. He often reminded us never to forget all we had.

In some ways, I decided I agreed with him. We did have food, though it was never "plenty" unless you counted holidays, which were spent at our grandparents. I was grateful for all we had. Thankfulness did not make this better though.

I grew up in a home that was safe and apart from the outside world. That was true, but it was also true that home was never a place I could express myself, not fully, even before I knew I was lesbian.

Dad was extremely religious, though he stopped attending church when we were little. I guess he had gotten into a disagreement with the clergy over the second commandment; he believed pictures of Jesus went against that commandment and he left the church forever. Everyday he set time aside to pray with the family, at meals and on his own. He taught us what the Bible said, at least what it said according to him. Same-sex couples were not a topic, most probably, because he just didn't believe it could exist in his own home. He died before he knew about me. He was a hard man and I never missed him. He was devoted but lacked love for his family. He taught me Jesus loved me but he never taught me he loved me. I think I could have used the love from both.

Mom had fully accepted me when I came out. After I'd grown up and moved away, she seemed much happier. I always thought it was simply because I had moved away. If I wasn't needing her, her life was easier. She was supportive and even loved the kids but we were never close. She just wasn't that sort of mom. We weren't that sort of family.

I think I grew up craving love and guidance denied me. When we had our children, I showed them every day how much I loved them; how happy they made my life. I taught them Jesus loves them but I hugged them every chance I saw.

I went home. I needed a nap. I *wanted* a nap.

I was surprised to find the next couple of days easy. I didn't question myself or my decisions. I hadn't even realized how often I'd plagued Sarah with little things until she texted to ask if I was feeling alright.

Surprised, I'd texted back, 'Yes, doing great, why?'

She answered, 'Oh good. You normally just text to tell me you are filling up your car, or buying milk. Or if you want your hair done, or anything. You haven't asked me anything yesterday or today. For anything. Smiley face.'

That text made me stop and really evaluate some things and myself.

It seemed I had given over complete control because I did not trust myself enough to know if I should even buy something as small as milk. I think I'd done that at least in the beginning to make sure we had enough in our account for everything. Since I didn't work, I had felt for a long time that the money was mostly Sarah's.

"She worked really hard," I told myself over and over.

I minimized my own hard work because it was simple chores. A few days before, I witnessed a tough scene from my own childhood where I'd learned chores were menial and difficult. Worse, I saw how I'd been taught I did mundane chores badly.

No wonder I didn't trust myself with the bigger things. How sad.

My adult self saw this much differently, of course. Chores are not always fun, but they certainly are needed. For Heaven's sake, people eat every day. We wear clothes every day. At some point, we have to take care of those things. Everyone does. Every single person has to do, take care of themselves and what they use daily. I had never ever thought that thought before.

Thanks to those childhood experiences, I'd sentenced myself to a lifetime of doing other people's chores. I really believed it was my role to make their lives easier and therefore, happier through sacrifice. My role as a daughter had been caretaker of my parents, their house, and my sister. I just widened that role to include my wife and children as I aged. I now understood I wasn't taking up too much space or taking away from others through being.

It was time to visit the therapist again.

"So, how was these two days, did you remember more?" per her normal manner, she started before I sat myself down.

"Well when I saw that child, who was me, getting talked to like that, I realized a few things, I guess."

All of a sudden, I grew nervous talking to her about this. Thanks to Dad, I had never talked poorly about our childhood or home life. Not ever.

"Hmmm, yes, well, what did you see?" she waited patiently while I crossed and uncrossed my legs. I pulled my jacket onto my legs, then up to my shoulders. I shook my hair loose from between my neck and couch. She only waited.

"I guess, well, I walked into our house. I haven't been there in years. Not since way before mom died. She sold it not long after dad died and moved to her own smaller place. Our old home was perfect with no dust or grime anywhere," I paused, seeing the white walls again, "I did as you suggested, I went to my old room. I looked around, and saw me when I was seven or so." I paused again, seeing the little scene, "See, it was Friday. Fridays were our cleaning days. I tried to help. My sister, she never liked cleaning, so I did her share and she played with her friends. I tried but…"

My voice faded a little as the scene evolved. I found it difficult to tell the next part, "My mother was standing in front of me; she was really angry with how I'd cleaned the bathroom and left this dust on my dolls' dresses." I felt so silly, this was just a dumb memory, and I didn't want to sound like I was whining. Still, my voice caught seeing it again. I truly felt pain at having caused my mother distress and more work. I felt ashamed, small, and vulnerable. I wanted her to be happy. I wanted her to have her space and time. This scene proved I was too much work, an embarrassment to an otherwise clean home. My dolls were dusty on a shelf, darkening her reputation as a wife and mother. I felt awful for creating her anger. I looked the dolls over in my mind again as shame rose like bile in my throat. I caused her so much grief.

And yet, how could I have done so? I was so little in this memory.

I heard rather than felt my next words. My voice sounded small, far away, "You see, there was an attachment for the vacuum that was made to dust curtains or dresses. I guess I didn't know about it, anyways, I'd never used it." I stopped. When I said this out loud, it just sounded dumb. Like I was whining.

"You are not whining. What did you learn?" her question caught me off-guard. How did she always know what I was thinking?

"Well, I did as you suggested. I looked at me as a child. I was always told how chubby I was but I wasn't that bad, actually. I saw my hair next. I was always told to fix it, that it just hanged on me. Looking at it now, it wasn't that bad either. I was just a kid. How perfect was I supposed to look? As I looked at myself as a child, I realized how differently I have raised my own children. I didn't expect those things from them. Her house was perfect, absolutely perfect. And you know? It never made anyone happy. I thought she was never happy and I thought that was my fault. I guess it wasn't though. It couldn't have been. I was just too small for that to be true."

My voice grew stronger, louder with each thought.

She nodded, "Ah, yes. Well, as children, we often adopt responsibility for things that are simply not required of children. We see unhappy parents and we believe if we can get the grades or do the chores, they will be happy. But that is not the case. Often, it has nothing to do with the child and the child only learns to be overly critical of themselves. What more did you learn?"

I took a deep breath, "I think both of them were just unhappy with their lives. Dad was so religious, he was unkind. Maybe he was unkind to her. She wanted everyone to think we were the perfect family. And Dad never let us sayspeak one word against either of them. You know, the commandment, *obey your mother and father*…I always just understood I took from them, there was no way they could take from me. After all I took from their table and any fun they might have. It was me who kept them from saving; not their own recklessness. I took happiness from them. I couldn't tell anyone about it. I never could explain the weight I felt."

I realized I wasn't breathing, so I forced down a gulp or two.

"Seeing this memory today though, I saw an innocent, naive child, someone who was just learning, just trying to be good. She was not failing. It was them who were failed her. I picked her up and I brought her away from there. I told her she didn't have to stay there and believe those things anymore."

I felt a couple of tears hot on my face, so I brushed them away.

"Mmmhm. And how have the last couple of days been? Have you had any more memories?"

She watched me carefully.

"Well, yes, here and there. I have."

"Very normal. You see, you are here, mid-life fast approaching. Your life's work was to undo all this trauma that had been done to you. You raised happy, loving children. You experienced a good marriage. Now, what do you do? Those things are done, you finished them. It was almost easy for you to do those things while you ignored your own painful memories, perhaps *so* you could ignore those painful memories. And now, the mid-life is sneaking up on you, you grieve for the not-so-distant past and are facing your own trauma, because you no longer need to suppress it. You have time and even if you didn't invite this, the universe has deemed it so."

I thought quietly about what she was saying. I knew what she said was all truth. Here I was, at the age I was, trying to move on from some really happy years. My babies were everything to me; they filled my days. And even though I had lost myself to them, I couldn't say it wasn't worth it. I couldn't believe those days were over and done. Just thinking it made me gasp, my heart filled with such a pain that physically hurt. I couldn't hold back a torrent of tears.

"You are grieving, just as if you lost a loved one. That is normal. Even though no one talks about this loss, it is a loss. It is the loss of what you built, what you loved. Yes, you are lucky you got to raise your children, yes, many people experience shorter years. This does not make you ungrateful. This is a loss. You dedicated your *life*, maybe even your *soul* to your family for many years. And now, things have changed. That is a loss. It is real and until you go through the grieving cycle, you will not be able to fully move forward in your own life. Do you know the steps for grief?"

She pulled a pamphlet from one of the many piles surrounding her.

"Death means a change. If we lose someone to death, we are losing them in this physical life. That is a change, isn't it? Where once we could hold them, hug them, that is no more. That life, the one before now, you are losing it. It will change. Just like a death, you cannot get those years back again. They are gone for good."

I swallowed hard at her words but I looked into her eyes.

"You cannot re-experience those years. Even if you were to produce another baby, things would not be the same or bring back those years you raised Jordan and Chloe. You know that and you can accept that. That is the second step. You can stop not wanting to believe those years are done. You can accept this new chapter."

I nodded while I sobbed. My shoulders heaved with the pain of closing this chapter of my life. I knew it was time, but I wasn't ready for it to close. I guess somethings we don't get to decide. I forced myself to breathe the way she taught me just a few weeks prior and I put the pamphlet into my bag.

"You are experiencing pain right now, from your loss and your gained awareness. You are now aware why you have thought the way you do, why you worked so hard to raise your family the way you have, and all this is painful. You can accept these growing pains. Accept the loss and the gain," she patted my arm, "Let's schedule for next week."

9

The next few days were easier. I still felt the deep sorrow of losing my children's childhoods to growing up. I still felt a little raw from the memory I experienced so vividly in her office. I also felt lighter. The burdens that had been so heavy for too long were still there. They hadn't magically disappeared but through acknowledging them, they had become lighter. I think I grew stronger, too. Lighter burdens shouldered by new strength made them almost weightless.

Time had forced a healing onto my soul that I still was learning to trust. It had also given me the faith to continue healing. I wanted Sarah to know how much I loved her, how much I appreciated her hard work. I felt as if I had acted selfishly and I wanted to contribute to our family again. I wanted me to make my wife's life beautiful and easier again.

The therapist had advised I give myself time and love. If I wanted to nap, I should nap. If I wanted to go out for a walk, I should. She wanted me to practice listening to what I wanted and then to act on it. One afternoon, I found myself craving some tea and wanting to look over an old book.

Even though I felt a little silly, I pulled our dog-eared copy of *Winnie the Pooh* by A.A. Milne down. I wiped a tear away as I recalled just how many times, I'd read this dear book aloud to Jordan and Chloe. I opened it to the middle and saw Pooh stuck in Rabbit's front door. The simple illustrations still tugged at my heart where the delicate colors filling in the simple grass and dirt that made up Rabbit's front door.

I read the little chapter right up to when they finally freed the silly old bear. I shut the book and drank the rest of my tea thinking. Funny, I'd read that book so many times and never thought too much about any meaning beyond lovely little stories. Now I had time to think and it really hit me how much that bear loved himself while he stayed humble. There was no reference to him feeling overly bad for getting stuck in his friend's front door because he was too fat. Instead he'd expressed regret about missing some lunches. Even though his friend was not happy with the situation of losing the use of his front door, he had never once shamed him either. He didn't enable him either. Rabbit made him stick to his diet. Pragmatic rabbit knew Pooh couldn't stay there forever. He simply helped him meet a goal.

I put the book away and took my cup to the kitchen. I poured myself some more tea, a little lost in my own thoughts. The idea that Pooh never seemed to bothered about his weight or his desire for honey refused to leave me alone. I was amazed he wasn't worried about eating too much. I had always worried about food and not simply to watch my weight.

I was afraid I was taking away from someone else or taking more than my share. I paused in front of the mirror that decorated the hallway and I forced myself to look at my reflection. I saw what I normally saw, the mom body. The sagging breasts, that pooch that refused to recess. Then I saw the expression on my face, the disapproval. Why couldn't I be more like Pooh? I decided it was time to try.

I put my hands on my belly, I felt them there, warm and capable. I took a deep, cleansing breath. I meditated on the fact my precious babies had started life beneath my cupped hands in that little pooch. I rubbed it a little, remembering how they'd moved, how big I'd gotten with each of them. I looked up and saw my face reflecting back at me. I was smiling. There was no longer disapproval as I looked down at my own body.

"What did you do today, Mom?" Chloe leaned over and kissed my cheek while Jordan shooed me out of the driver's seat.

I gladly traded with him. He was a good driver, even though he now only had his license for a few days. I watched him out the corner of my eye, he buckled in, and adjusted his mirrors. He looked all around, then slowly pulled into traffic. All his attention was on the road.

"Well, I enjoyed some tea and read an old favorite. Then the usual. I did some laundry, started dinner. How was your day?"

Chloe went on and on about the happenings of her day, it filled the rest of the ride home. I was happy to see Sarah had come home while I picked up the kids. We went inside.

"So what book did you read, Mom?" Jordan asked as we entered the kitchen. Sarah was already serving everyone up dinner.

I kissed her on the cheek, "What a treat, thanks!"

I sat down and waited for Sarah to join us. I told them how I had pulled the old favorite down and what I discovered about that bear.

"You know, Mom, that is true. I think all the animals, even Eeyore loved themselves there. Even he just seemed to acknowledge he could be sad," Jordan said.

"And Tigger! Even when he trampled all over rabbit's garden, he didn't go around begging everyone to forgive him. He just sorts of expected it after he told them he was sorry. I don't think he even stayed to help, and they still all loved him," Chloe's input was sweet.

"I never read that book as much as you guys," Sarah chimed in, "But I think you're right. There are some great lessons hidden in there, aren't there?"

She squeezed my hand, "I'm glad you took the time to read that today."

Her and the kids jumped up to begin clearing the dishes away. They were headed to a hockey game in an hour. I wasn't going.

They finished much more quickly than I would have, had I done them on my own. Then they filed out each kissing me on the cheek. I heard the front door close behind them. I peeked out the window, Jordan was driving again.

Sarah had told me she was glad I'd taken the time to read the book. I think she meant it, too. I decided to go ahead and just read the rest of it. I was distracted though. I put the book down and listened to the empty house.

It was almost purely silent. No shouts. No laughter. No blaring music. No water running. Nothing. The day had been pretty silent, too. Sitting there, I felt at peace. Nothing was calling for me to finish it, no chore needed my attentions. No one needed me.

I guess this was part of accepting the next part of my life. It would be quieter. I thought about that for a few moments and was surprised no fresh tears fell. The pain in my chest was there, but it was neither heavy nor sharp. I guess this was the acceptance stage.

I realized, sitting there in the quiet, how angry I'd felt when Sarah announced her retirement. I wasn't ready for our children to be the ages they were or Sarah and I to be at the ages we now were. I wasn't sure how to move on and between the fear and pain of losing my youth, I'd experienced anger at time leaving me. Life had gone too quickly and when I'd realized that, I feared it. Anger always comes from fear.

Sitting here in the quiet, I realized time is constant and moves the same for all of us. I wasn't angry anymore. I wasn't even that sad. I wasn't afraid. I might not be cartwheeling over this particular threshold of my life, but I believed I was ready, at last, to at least step over it.

I did realize I didn't want to have so much quiet though. It was too much. I liked a noisy house filled with life and I wasn't ready to trade that for quiet. I turned the T.V. on and I remembered my old aunt. I didn't have grandparents and she filled that role. Her T.V. was *always* on. Now I knew why.

My life changed dramatically over the next few days. I felt lighter, stronger and though I still tired easily, I found my mind was calmer. Sometimes, I felt down but it no longer entrapped me. I felt as if I could manage. Life was definitely looking up.

10

I wanted to be happier, I wanted to move on, free from the past patterns that had so haunted me. I did everything just as the therapist advised and accepted life for what it was, instead of fighting it. Perhaps that is why I was more energetic; I wasn't battling all day every day.

One day as I got out of my shower, I dared look into the mirror. The same aging woman looked back but she looked a little less dilapidated than before. I don't believe I was imagining things either. I had been walking every day and it showed. I walked straighter, keeping my core tucked in and shoulders straight. I applied lotion to my arms, then my legs, and took out the hair dryer. I dressed and walked into the kitchen. Chloe was there and I kissed her cheek.

"Wow, Mom! You look great, what did you do with your hair?" she asked as I entered.

"I didn't do anything, love," and I kissed her cheek again.

It was time to see the therapist and this time, I felt armed walking inside. I had made a small list of what I wanted to work on and kept it tucked in my arm as I settled into the most comfortable spot on the couch.

"Tell me how you have been," the therapist in her usual fashion, not bothering to wait for me to get comfortable.

"I have been doing better," I couldn't hide the pleasure from my voice. I was working hard and I was proud of my progress, "I made a list of things I think I need to work on or work towards and I wrote down some questions."

She didn't say a word, but smiled a little and raised her eyebrow.

I took out the list. The first thing read, "Is depression like addiction? Is this something I will need to watch or recover from my entire life?" Just saying the words quickened my heart rate, just a little. I didn't really want to fight this forever. The thought scared me just a little.

"Interesting question. I haven't thought about it being like addiction. Certainly, a recovering addict must always be vigilant. Depression and anxiety might be a little bit like that, especially if you feel they have haunted you for a long time or many years?"

I nodded to her query.

"I think it is safe to say you might always need to watch yourself or at least understand you are sensitive to it. It can certainly cycle around, thanks to hormones and the like as well."

I nodded. I wasn't surprised, even though I was a little disappointed. My next line read, "Are some people just more than others?"

"That is interesting, I am going to assume you are comparing yourself to someone. There is no need to do that. We are all here, all in our moments, beginning from many places, and we all have unique experiences shaping our beliefs, our memories. I do not think it is necessary or even wise to compare."

I told her about reading the *Winnie the Pooh* by A.A. Milne the last week, "You know, I learned something, reading those simple stories of a child's imagination in a tiny corner of a made-up world. I learned I don't need to be thin or even all that kind to earn my place in this life. I think it's more like I exist and that is enough. For years, starting when I was so small, I learned to make people happy through sacrificing my own happiness, my own wants. I wanted to earn their love and earn the right to be around them. But that was wrong, wasn't it?"

The therapist waited for me to collect my thoughts. She knew I knew the answer and waited for it.

"I never, ever thought of Sarah as earning her right to be in this world. I never thought of my children like that either. It was only me that had to earn my place. As I was reading those simple stories, I realized I had never needed to do anything to earn that right. The bear was happy with himself even though he was round. His friends all had different struggles and yet, as they all lived their together, none made any of the others feel as if they did not belong. At least, not for long. I think or at least the other day, I thought I need to adopt that idea towards myself."

The therapist nodded and confessed, "I have never read those little stories, but I believe I shall put that on my list for next week." She wrote *Winnie the Pooh* down on a free piece of paper.

"After last week, I remembered a few things that really made me quite a part of me for a very long time. It makes me sad I shushed the part of me that allowed me to enjoy life. It seems so clear; looking back as to why I have thought the way I did, yet it seems unfair. You said I was grieving for the life I lost as I turn towards a new chapter and you were right.

The reason I was grieving was back then when I was raising my babies, I felt so needed, so loved. No matter what we did, no matter if our days were great or a little hard, we loved each other. I felt as if I were really earning my place in this life. And as that has changed, my role has evolved in their lives, I felt as if there was nothing more to do, there was nothing before me. Without being needed, I was not earning my place in life and if I couldn't earn it, that meant I didn't belong."

The therapist listened intently. I could feel new tears sliding down my cheeks but my voice was steady.

"Sarah got promoted through her hard work many times. Then she announced she was ready to retire and I just felt as if what I had done just didn't compare. I didn't know what to do. I doubted I could work again, at least not in the same capacity as before. Then yesterday, I just had a thought sort of fall into my head. I didn't need to do anything more, there was nothing to prove. I have lived. I have loved. I have raised my children. If that is all I have done, that would be enough. After thinking that, I feel better."

"So, you are saying you have realized no matter what you do simply by living, you are doing enough that life is not earned?"

She said it far more simply than my thoughts had played it out and she said it with little conviction. I wondered if I somehow got that wrong.

"Or maybe no? When I thought it yesterday, it felt so right? I guess if that were true though, there wouldn't be filled prisons or down-beaten people."

I forced myself to breath the long slow breaths.

"Or maybe those people have chosen their paths at least to some degree. You cannot compare yourself to them or their actions. You, of course, have been given chances in life many miss out on. Perhaps though, it is the person missing out on their worth, blinding them from seeing such chances. I think even in your darkest hours, you wanted to believe in your own worth. Is that right?"

I nodded.

She went on, "You are right. If we all understood our own worth, we would see and live remarkably. There would be no reason to act against what is meant for us and that is the fact we are supposed to enjoy life.

Yes, we suffer. We are only human but there are many things to enjoy in this life and adopting the belief we are unworthy or that our suffering will somehow pay-off is simply untrue."

"We are only human and adopting the belief we are unworthy of happiness?" I said her words back to her and she nodded, "Or that our suffering will somehow pay-off is simply untrue." I took in a deep breath. I thanked her for her time and asked to make an appointment in a week. Even though the appointment had been short, I wanted to think about all she'd said, all I had said.

When I got home, I parked the car but I didn't walk inside. Instead I walked towards the nearby park that I had so frequented lately. My mind was wandering a little.

I was grieving my own past and I wanted to come to terms with what I had stolen from myself before I went home.

As I walked, I thought about the last few months and what I dared allow myself to remember from years I thought I'd forgotten. The wisdom by therapist imparted on me was two-fold. The first is how our past drives us. The second is the fact that we can change that.

I found a secluded bench and sat down. The child I'd encountered during that session had surprised me. I recalled vividly, constantly being told my hair was not fixed or that I was chubby. Most often, it was that I didn't do chores correctly. Until I revisited that scene, I had buried not only that scene but hundreds just like it. Growing up, I thought our home was normal. I never questioned how I was treated.

Even after I had my own children, I never once gave credit to myself for being nice to them. I was because I loved them. I loved their messy, un-brushed morning hair. I loved watching them learn and teaching their little hands to do things. I loved hearing their childish thoughts and dreams and off-key songs. God bless her, Chloe still sang off-key and I still loved listening.

All I had done though, pushing those memories down without ever validating them, was lie to myself. My childhood was not nightmarish but it also was not good. I grew into a young woman afraid to make mistakes, so I didn't try new things. As I grew even older, that doubt grew grounding me into a worthless individual nearly incapable of making any decisions.

It saddened me to recall the twenty-five year old contemplating a haircut to ensure her hair wasn't just hanging on her head. Then talking herself out of it because she couldn't make her mind up which cut would look best. I wanted to tell her she was missing the point. Her hair was gorgeous, long, lush, and a little wild. If she cut it, it would just grow back.

I thought of the same young woman walking into a fitness class right up to the door, seeing all the in-sync women inside with flat tummies and almost running away. She felt she didn't compare. I wished now I could tell her all of them had all been beginners at some point. They hadn't always been in sync. They'd worked hard to get into shape, but all had started from somewhere.

I watched as she saw the love of her life for the first time. That beautiful woman had walked up to the coffee counter, back straight, head high, and ordered something not on the menu. She didn't apologize, didn't ask if they could, she simply ordered and received. When she walked out, she didn't trip, didn't rush. That perfect hair swished right out with her and of course, there was the young woman staring after her, feeling completely unworthy of any attentions someone like that might have for her. I wish I could tell her to go after her, she was just what that other woman was searching for.

I thought of the younger, tween version of me and nearly cried. I had the same messy hair, still wasn't doing chores properly. And by now, I'd discovered how attracted I was to other girls. I couldn't tell anyone ever. I would be turned out of house and home. I secluded myself a bit more and missed out on lots of normal high-school stuff. I never went to prom or any other dances. I wish I could tell that young woman there would come a time for her to shine.

I couldn't tell the past me anything and I grieved for the younger me a little while longer. She had missed out on so much and in the end, that seclusion and suffering only brought on the shell of the woman I faced a few months ago. I would never tell Chloe or Jordan to simply stop building themselves. If they stopped now, they wouldn't have anything in a few years. Yet, I had robbed myself of just that through adopting the false beliefs of leftover hurts from a scarred childhood. And here I sat.

I knew I was at a significant crossroads in my life. Just like the therapist told me, midlife was waiting for me, watching me just from around the next corner. Even though I had neglected myself almost totally for many, many years, I had the power to change. I could pick up right now with what I had or I could do what I'd tried a few weeks ago. I didn't have to go on and I knew everyone would get through. After all, people survive, even thrive, remarkable circumstances.

I thought about the crossroads I was facing and looked long and hard down each. I did not see any suffering for myself down one, short road. The other side was dark, I couldn't see where it led. I looked and looked and realized the difference between the two.

I could only see the end down the one lane because *it was short.*

And that made all the difference in the world.

I couldn't see the end of the other, it was dark, and yet, I was curious about it. I was curious where it would end and what I might see on the way. I couldn't know the future, no one can, but I knew I wanted to find out what it held. I stood up and stretched, it had gotten dark and chilly while I was out. I turned to go home and almost ran smack into my wife and kids. I was shocked to see them, I hadn't known they'd walked up behind me.

I hugged them hard, pulling all of us in tight together and I laughed. The universe had just presented me with remarkable clarity of the future, of my future. I couldn't see everything, but there were pleasant surprises in store.

11

After such clarification, I was surprised at how tired I felt over the next week. I had made my choice. I even took the first difficult step down the dark path that led to my future. I reminded myself of my choice every morning. I woke up each day and drank a glass of water. I made sure I dressed and readied myself for the day. I still felt tired. And that led to disappointment.

As I cleaned the kitchen, I thought of the many books and films I had enjoyed over the years. I realized most of them did not show realistic emotional or mental healing. *I guess that wouldn't be interesting to watch endless days of a sad person wandering around lost,* I thought, the next thought quickly followed, *It would take too long, can't fit all this into two hours or a couple hundred pages.*

The truth was healing was taking a lot longer than I ever thought it would or could. I was doing good, I knew that. I hadn't had too many dark thoughts since the day in the park. Truth was, I still felt down sometimes. I still felt anxious. I still texted Sarah a lot. I decided it was a good thing I had my next appointment that afternoon.

This time, I didn't wait for her to begin asking questions. Instead I hugged her and before I sat, I asked, "Does it always take this long for people to heal?"

She raised her eyebrows, "Hello, Jess, I am fine, how are you?" She laughed a little, "You know, I believe it takes all different people different times to heal. We all come to it at different points and depending on that, how long we suffered, how much we suffered dictates healing time."

I felt myself frowning. I hadn't wanted to hear that. I'd hoped she would tell me how to speed up the process or to point out how I was holding myself back.

"Be gentle with yourself, Jess. You are healing. You are doing really well and I am so proud of you. This takes time though. Think about it logically, our brains are born clean, no memories stored. And we learn by storing actions, impressions, and events. As we grow and encounter new situations, our brains revert to those memories guiding our actions and emotions. You are rewriting that, it took you how many years to establish this working memory? It will take time. Not as long as before, but it will take time. You have done the first step remarkably well; gaining awareness. Perhaps it was Sarah announcing her retirement, but something triggered your awareness of your discomfort with your current situation."

I looked at her deep into her eyes, "Do you think I am jealous of my wife?"

"Before we figure that out, I want you to ask yourself why were so uncomfortable with your current situation to erupt like you did. Something caused that, was it simply living as you did for so long? Or was it the time line Sarah put out for you?"

I thought about what she said, it actually took me a few minutes to sort my feelings. What exactly *had* happened?

"You know, I think it was both. Sarah announced her retirement rather grandly at dinner one night. She was so proud of herself, so excited to take the next step. She never told me about her plans or what might happen that week at work. She never really has, you know. She always has kept work at work and home at home. Oh, I knew when things were going well or bad, but it was like seeing the tip of an iceberg. You know I think I felt left out. She didn't even ask if I was ready."

As I thought about that night, I realized how hurtful her actions were. She hadn't consulted me, not at all, on when was best for us to make our next move. I went on.

"I really think I felt left out and unimportant. She keeps saying "our," but really it is her move. My life might not change at all. I will still have the kids, still have the house. She keeps saying she will be there for me, but honestly, I doubt my day to day will change much. I *will* enjoy having her around, of course. I love being with her but this move is hers. It's not mine."

The therapist nodded.

"I really think that made me revaluate most of my life. If Sarah retires, what exactly does that even mean? What do I do differently? Our home has always been pretty divided and not badly. She went to work, I took care of the house. If she is home, she normally takes the children, I take the house." I sighed. My chest felt tight.

"And? Do you really want to take the house?" the therapist was so direct with her questions today.

I hadn't really thought about that before. I liked our house. I liked it being clean, organized. I wanted the kids to know the value of taking care of their things but deep down, if I dared admit, I didn't really enjoy doing the chores all the time.

"I guess you're right again. If I can admit it, I don't enjoy doing the chores on my own. I am not saying that no one helps but the planning and carrying out is pretty much up to me. And if I admit it, I don't want to keep doing that. I always thought I was doing it for the kids and Sarah but to be honest, I'm not sure they notice or care so much. I mean, of course, it is completely easy for them to have clean clothes, an organized bathroom, and dinner ready but I don't want to keep doing this. Not like this."

I couldn't believe how much lighter I felt saying those words out loud.

"If Sarah retires, I don't want to just pick up while she goes out and does whatever she wants. I mean, is that fair? I want something more from here as well."

The therapist took a deep breath and watched me for a few moments.

"You know, we had the children, of course, that was my idea, Sarah told me she hadn't really thought of it. She was completely on board," I looked into the therapist's eyes, "She just had never planned on it, she said she never thought she would meet anyone she would want to have children with. I guess it was easy to divide our lives like that. I don't think anyone took advantage of me, I just did it, and now it is just like that. I remember my grandparents; she always cleaned and was busy around the house. He ran for town council, he fished, he visited his friends, and hosted poker night. She never missed a Sunday in church. That was her out. If I am honest, even as a child, her life sort of scared me. I didn't want to be like that, to end up like her. When Sarah retires, I don't want *my* life to carry on just like this. I would like a change, too, I hope for a change. Except. Our kids aren't going to be grown, it won't be time for me to retire. And then what? Sarah comes home, she's the fun one. She's the one who keeps the kids going to their sports, even if I end up running them to the practices. She gets to go to the games, cheering them on. When people meet her, they are enamored with her. I heard just the other day at one game, another mother talking with her."

I said all of it very fast, almost as if I thought about it too much, I wouldn't say what I felt.

The therapist didn't say anything for a moment. Then, "You know it is alright, you know, to not love cleaning up after everyone. You said your mother was very particular with your childhood home? What is it like caring for your own home?

I chewed my lip as I thought about how to answer her question. I certainly liked my home being clean rather than cluttered. I liked clean laundry. I told her as much.

"I think my home is completely different from where I grew up. I don't demand as much from my children or Sarah. Our home is clean but not pristine and I think that I prefer it that way."

She frowned in my direction a little, "Jess, when you tell me you don't demand as much from your family, where do you place those demands?"

She raised her eyebrows in my direction.

I lifted my chin. I didn't have to answer; she and I both knew I placed those demands onto myself. I didn't say anything.

"Take a deep breath, just like you've been doing. Let your shoulders relax a little," she directed more than advised and I did as I was told. It felt good to let my shoulders down. I breathed easier.

"That's better, now tell me the truth. Are you jealous of your wife?"

I tilted my head back onto the sofa and closed my eyes. *Was I?* I wondered.

I thought of Sarah, there was certainly a lot *to* envy. She was extremely fit. She was beautiful. She was respected by both women and men. I knew she was hit on often by both as well. I couldn't remember the last time anyone but her had admired me or complimented me. Let alone hit on me. I certainly wasn't respected by my peers.

"I don't know. The other day, we were at Jordan's game, and another mother approached her. Now, most parents are polite when I am there. No one is rude, at least not to my face, but no one is really friendly either. Anyways, we both were there and this woman approached Sarah. She told her how brave she thought she was, how proud she was of her. She admired her sacrifices she made for our family, "Stepping outside traditional roles." Sarah was gorgeous about it, of course she thanked her and told her it took both of us to raise our family. The whole incident bothered me though. No one has ever approached me like that. Not once. I just sat there wondering why and if what I had done was unnoticeable. It made me question myself, what Sarah really thinks of me and how the children see me."

"I don't do a lot of couples counseling, but I do know this is pretty common in all relationships, straight, same sex. It doesn't matter. There always seems to be one partner who takes on more of the house and the other takes on the professional world. There is jealousy between both for obvious reasons. One feels left out while they work, one feels left out of the career world. And this is the same in most families at one point or another, even when both partners work outside the home."

I nodded, that made sense. "I don't think I am jealous of Sarah, but there is a lot to be jealous of, she is gorgeous. Her body isn't scarred by stretch marks, nothing sags. She is quite a catch. I think I am not jealous but I sometimes wonder about how we look together. I get a lot of looks that tell me people wonder how we two could be together. When we are together on our own, I don't feel that though."

"Is she jealous of you?"

I shook my head, "No, I don't think so. I mean, why?"

The therapist didn't answer my question, instead she said, "Well, perhaps it is time you start thinking like that instead of what more she has to offer versus you. You are quite a catch. You are loyal, you are beautiful, you are kind." She went on, "You are intelligent and creative. Do you believe these things about yourself?"

I took a deep breath. I didn't know if I believed them or not, did anyone believe those things about themselves? I asked that question aloud, "Does anyone believe those things about themselves?"

"Sarah does," the therapist didn't even pause to think.

I left soon after that, I had plenty to think about. This time, I'd been given homework. I walked into the house a little tired. I could hear Jordan and Chloe arguing in the kitchen.

"Just do it, stop being a dumb-ass," Jordan's voice was angry.

"I don't want to, I never liked cleaning the sink? Because I am a girl?" Chloe sounded close to tears.

"Don't be stupid, Mom told us to take care of things better, you know. You remember, stop being stupid and acting as if you don't remember, when she tried that,

that night, well she told us to help her more," Jordan's voice was full of frustration.

"Why did she though? It can't be hard staying in all day, she doesn't volunteer or anything. Mom goes out to work, she does alright. Mommy doesn't have to do anything. Why did she try that, Jordan?" Chloe wasn't being mean but her words stabbed into my heart.

Jordan sighed, "I don't know. Maybe she is just getting older and doesn't like it."

I stepped into the kitchen and they turned guiltily in my direction.

My voice was soft, "I didn't plan it and I am trying to figure out why and how I got there."

Chloe looked horrified that I overheard them. Jordan looked sad.

I felt my shoulders drop as I answered what they said as honestly as I could, "No one likes to age, no one likes to realize parts of life are passing by or over. I don't think I have a huge problem with that, but I do miss what we had a few years ago. I was actually grieving for a part of my life, and of yours that is over. I think I am accepting that now."

I was hurt. I was hurt because I think somewhere deep down, I had hoped these two beautiful souls hadn't noticed how off I was. I hoped I hadn't hurt them through my actions and subsequent healing time. Here was the proof that scared me the most. They had noticed and I had hurt them. I wasn't sure what I could do to un-hurt them. I tried not to listen to the biggest fear of all, "What if I can't un-hurt them?"

I walked over and I took my precious children in my arms. I felt their pain, something they had bottled up for the past few weeks. I had deluded myself through false hope they were not hurt. I was wrong. I had to fix this, at least as best as I was able.

We stayed in that little huddle for a long time. Jordan was first to pull back. He had tears on his face and the cost of him spilling those hurt my heart. Chloe used the back of his shirt to dry her eyes.

I tried to stop crying, couldn't so I told myself, *Let it out. That is what you want, and need right now.*

Then I tried, like hell, to believe those words.

Finally, a good two or three full minutes later, I took a deep breath in and whispered, "I am so sorry. I have a lot of pain from a long time ago that I am trying to work through. It might be too soon or it might be too late, but I want to ask you to forgive me. Please forgive me for embarrassing your mother."

"Mommy, I was so afraid you wouldn't come home. That's all," Chloe's voice was so quiet, I had to lean in to hear.

"I just want you to be alright, mommy," Jordan's voice was soft, almost soft as Chloe's.

I nodded. I didn't feel deserving of their love, not after how I'd hurt them but I was teaching myself to think differently. I took another deep breath. And another.

I forced myself to smile and tell them thank you. I took a hand in each of mine.

"I don't feel like I deserved that, not so quickly," my voice cracked and more tears.

"Oh, mommy. Think of Tigger. We just talked about it the other day. No matter how many times he bounced everyone or messed up Rabbit's garden, he expected his friends to forgive him," Chloe's voice was so sweet, it was still childish but growing.

"Be Tigger, Mom. We can't stop loving you," Jordan squeezed my hand.

In those moments, in the warmth of our kitchen, my heart mended a little more. I realize no parent, not even myself or Sarah, could ever protect our children from all the pain in the world. I had introduced them to a very real pain just a few weeks ago.

Thank God, I'd survived that, because I just now introduced them to healing.

I felt closer to the kids than possibly ever. I was no longer the mommy on the pedestal. They'd seen me at my most human, most vulnerable, and yet, we grew closer through that pain. My heart actually felt newly healed and I thought this new healing had even healed some of the old hurt I'd carried for so long.

My mind was clearer than it had been in a long time. I woke each day not with a plan written in stone so much, but a feeling of purpose that was outside and more than simply dropping my children off to school or running their errands. I continued my walking each day and when I felt low, I simply breathed in and gave that feeling the space it was demanding right then.

I made dinner one night, I think it was a Tuesday, it was something new and everyone enjoyed it. Sarah had gotten off just a little late, so I was already serving up when she'd walked in. After that last therapist appointment, I'd watched how I thought of my wife more. I wanted to see if I was, in fact, jealous of her.

I don't know how straight couples are with each other. I'd fallen for an amazing woman. The therapist had assured me all couples go through pivotal points where they feel jealousy or other ugly feelings towards their significant others. I wondered if same sex experienced jealousy towards each other more.

I watched my wife walk in and greet us. She reached for a bottle of wine and sat down with us, kissing each kid and me before she took her seat. She looked amazing as usual. Her white suit was still white, even after a long day. Not a hair was out of place and her make-up was still perfect. I saw her reach for her first bite and close her eyes at the good flavor, she really savored her food. Her mouth was one of the most beautifully sculpted mouths I still had ever seen. Ever.

"This is really great, Jess. What is it?" she smiled at me and patted my hand.

I told her all about how I'd picked out the fresh herbs right from the small garden in the back and reduced the sauce till it was just so. I watched her eyes as I spoke.

Not once did she lose interest in what I was saying. She genuinely was interested in my day and how I'd accomplished something so tasty for our meal that evening. She engaged with the kids the same way.

Sarah actually was perfect. She had a perfect career and she looked perfect most of the time. Her kids were excellent students, hardworking and caring people. She provided us with a lovely home and good food. She was fun and attentive. As I watched her talk with Chloe about an assignment due in French the next day, I realized two things about myself and my amazing wife.

I do believe I had been harboring some jealousy towards her for a long time, if I was honest. When we'd decided to have children, it wasn't even a choice or difficult decision. I was the one that wanted to carry them. Sarah never *said* she didn't want to but she had never volunteered either. It really was a non-issue. Having the babies was, of course, a whole different matter.

Carrying children ages us. It actually is really hard on our entire bodies. Our ligaments stretch in ways hardly imaginable, our hearts pump for two, and we don't even really catch up on sleep and rest until that child is eight years old. Nothing really just goes back either, there is no going back after having a child. At least not in my experience. Once I'd conceived, nothing about me was the same.

I thought of them first. I took care of myself a lot while I was carrying them, watching what I ate, drinking enough. When they were born, that self-care shifted into giving them care. My body was different, too. My tummy was always going to show that I'd had children. If I was discovered in three hundred years by some archeologist, the first thing they would see from my leftover bones was that I was a woman who had multiple children.

My clear thinking changed, too. I was a little scattered now as I tried to keep our home in order and track four people. I was busy all the time in my thoughts. I don't think that quite goes back either. It's like once you know some things you can't unlearn them.

Once you are a mom, you don't ever really un-mom.

My wife had not experienced some of those changes simply because she hadn't carried our babies. Her body was still the size three it had always been. She had the energy of a twenty year old. Her mind, though, it had changed much like mine had. She was a little more scattered, a little foggier some days. I don't believe it was quite to the same extent as I experienced but she showed signs of motherhood.

I think I was not jealous of her body or her looks. I wasn't even jealous of her fabulous career. The sacrifices I'd made mattered to me and to those I loved the most. I didn't hold those against Sarah. I think I was just a little jealous that she never lost herself to us. I was a little jealous of her strength and her ability to step from motherhood to career woman so easily.

As I thought those things, I realized I had chosen my sacrifices and I was proud of them. I did not need anything more in my life to bring me fulfillment. I'd done that. For me, being a stay-at-home mom was enough, which meant, I was enough.

All those years I had tried proving myself to myself and to our family weren't futile but weren't necessary. Simply by being me, I had proved myself. My shoulders actually released all tension as I thought these thoughts.

My lungs decompressed and my neck relaxed. I knew it and I understood it, my life was enough simply because I was me. I slept soundly, eight hours straight through that night.

I was so happy to tell my therapist all my new learning the next day. I practically bounced into her office. I was expecting to see my beautiful older but not old Japanese-American therapist already sitting when I went through that door. Instead, I was greeted by no one.

It felt different, even the air in there, but I ignored it and I sat down. For the first time in weeks, I got comfortable before I was asked anything, I laughed at that a little. I took out my phone to check my calendar, maybe I'd gotten the date wrong. I was on time, even the right day. I looked around and decided to wait a little while.

I noticed some of the clutter was gone and the strangeness in the air didn't go away. It just felt hollow, a little bit empty. I wondered how long I'd have to wait for her, I'd never waited before. After about five more minutes, maybe a little longer, someone put their head in the door.

"Oh, hello. You are the appointment I could not get a hold," the young man was polite but a little indifferent, "Yes, well, you cannot come here anymore to see her. She died two days ago. If you need anything for insurance, I can help you and if you have any outstanding bills, you will be mailed those invoices."

I just looked at him. He must have had the wrong place. I don't think my therapist had even been ill. I told him so.

"Well, I am sorry. I know many people love her, loved her. Well, she was ill, actually. She was diagnosed with ovarian cancer about six weeks ago. You're not the only one she didn't tell. She said she didn't want to live any differently than before and if there was really nothing that could be done for her, she would just get on with it. I am sorry. I knew her, too."

I gathered my things and left. I felt so empty. I tried to talk myself out of this new grief, this new loss.

I hadn't known her very long. In fact, I hardly *knew* her at all. I did know she had a family, there'd been pictures in her office. I never asked too much about her, after all, I was the one in therapy. She knew she was sick almost the duration of the time we'd been meeting. And never said a word.

I did notice she'd used a blanket the last two weeks but her office was a little chilly and I didn't put too much thought into that. I had no way of knowing she'd been battling cancer. She had her hair. She didn't appear sick. I still felt loss though. A big loss.

I'd hardly even thanked her for all she did for me.

The tears came at that thought. She had helped me so much and I never even said thank you. I couldn't now. I never would. It hurt to know she had been so ill and still so willing to help. I turned and looked at her office one more time. Nothing was changed, but everything was different there. She *knew* she was dying as she helped me overcome my suicide.

What does a person do with that sort of knowledge? With that sort of love?

A few days later, there was an announcement that arrived in our mail. A candle light vigil was going to be held in her honor the next evening for those that wanted to celebrate her life. I decided to go. Jordan had a game, so Chloe offered to accompany me.

It was chilly standing out there, waiting for our candles. It was crowded, too. I guess she'd known a lot of people. We signed a guest book and each of us picked out a candle. The young man who had dismissed me stood at the front and we all quieted to hear what he had to say.

"I want to thank everyone for coming out tonight to celebrate my mom. She didn't want a funeral or a fuss. After seeing so many people come the last week though, I decided we needed something. She was an extraordinary woman. She always helped where she could. She genuinely loved people and helping to ease pain," he raised his candle, "I love you, Mom. You gave me the best life anyone could ever ask." We all bowed in silence when his voice broke.

It took him a few minutes to recover. When he did, his voice was strong.

"My mother made time to help others, for her, it was a life-essential. When we were kids, she helped my friends if they needed anything, she helped their parents. And as we grew up, she reached out to more and more in our community. Her physical life is over, but she taught me we are never gone. We are all part of this wonderful universe; this magic of life and her spirit will always be."

A sob of pain escaped from someone in the crowd and he looked over to a young woman whose shoulders were heaving with the sorrow she felt, he continued, "Her legacy is love. I look out here and I see that. Thank you all for attending, if anyone wants to say anything more about my mother, please come up."

A few people stood and said a few things, thanking her for her help, sharing how desperately she would be missed. I kept my head bowed for most of it. This loss was heavy to bear, I felt as if I was only just learning to heal and my guide was cruelly taken.

"I didn't know this lady. It sounds like she was very kind though. I want to tell her thank you, somehow. She helped my mommy," I looked up in shock. My Chloe was standing there, so young but so brave. She went on, "My mommy was having a hard time, I don't know why. I don't think she even knows why. But this lady, she helped her. I just wanted everyone to know that even though she must have been feeling really sick, she still helped my mom." And she stepped away, wiping tears from her cheek.

What a gift. I hadn't known this was in store for myself or my children.

Our family didn't talk a lot about that night or my illness. Aside from the conversation in the kitchen, we had only touched on it here and there. I didn't know how to help my children heal as I tried to heal. I had been given a gift in the form of an extraordinary therapist and she reached out even from death to guide me. That gift was not lost to Chloe.

"I hope I didn't embarrass you, Mommy, I just wanted to say thank you. I didn't say what happened, just that she'd helped so much. I can see you miss her," Chloe tucked her arm into mine and leaned her head onto my shoulder while she spoke. I wrapped my arm around her.

"You know, Cho, I didn't know her very well at all. But, yes, I miss her so much."

Hot tears spilled down my cheeks and we turned and went back home.

I made us some tea when we got home, it was comforting to have something warm in my hands. I hoped I'd learned enough from my guide to keep moving forward. Tonight, I sure didn't feel like there had been enough time spent with that marvelous woman. I thought back to our brief relationship.

She was quiet, small, and not quite beautiful. Her hair was long and streaked with gray. She always wore it pulled back. She dressed simply; I couldn't recall not seeing in her anything but a gray shirt and black pants. I think they were even yoga pants. She was so insightful though. Her intuition led her to ask the most thought-provoking answers to uncover the truth of a life. She was unafraid to ask the wrong thing. I wondered if she was always like this or if the advancement of death had inspired her.

I guess it could be both, I mused. Everyone tonight certainly thanked her for the parts she had played in their lives. Perhaps, she'd always had these qualities and they only heightened with the threat of death. Facing my own death not so many weeks ago, I wondered what my legacy would be.

A few weeks ago, even facing death, I certainly did not think of my legacy. That would have been too lofty for me to contemplate; legacies were for the great. My thinking was slowly changing though. The more I contemplate this, the more grateful I was for a second chance at leaving a legacy. If I had left those few weeks ago, the only legacy I had wouldn't have even *known* they were my legacy.

They wouldn't have even known. That thought hit me like a punch to the gut.

All the years I worked for them, all my sacrifices for them would only have been lost to their pain.

Healing is an odd journey. Over the next days, my heart was heavy. I reminded myself again and again I was merely learning something new. It would take some time.

How odd, I thought one afternoon, all the time learning new things takes, but doesn't take. I had known her for such a short time yet, I'd come to rely on her for so much and so quickly.

Instinctively, I understood I was not going to find another therapist. I didn't want to. More than that, no one could ever fill her little shoes. I would have to find another way to endure this journey. Until I figured *that* out, I would just need to give myself some space and breath in this life.

Sarah texted me one morning, closer to noon. She said she was working late.

I read the text and re-read it. I took a little while to respond. It was strange, she hadn't really worked late in a long time and even if she did, she rarely let me know this early. For the rest of the day, I wondered what she was doing.

It was funny in a way, all these years I had never really felt much if she had to work late. In the beginning of our marriage, I had also worked. Then we had the babies. I learned, then, to really push down most of my feelings. I don't think I'd felt much of anything the past three or four years; I'd gotten so good at that. I wondered if that had showed. Then I wondered again why she'd texted.

I cleaned the kitchen and started some laundry. Then I checked my phone. There was nothing more, no explanation, no "have a nice day." Nothing. I think that day when I realized what I lost, that was even more painful than deciding it was time to die.

I'd had a love I'd always felt was out of reach, that I didn't deserve. I had turned off most of my feelings, trying to keep my sadness at bay. Now, I could hardly recall the last time I felt my heart flutter with the excitement of being in love. I hadn't even gotten excited last Christmas.

I sighed. I wasn't even sure how long I hadn't felt something. I hadn't fallen out of love with Sarah, I hoped she didn't think that, but I hadn't acted like I'd been in love for a long time. I wondered if all couples with children were like that. I wondered if all spouses went through something like this. Then I wondered if it was only me.

To heal, I needed a way forward. I needed some light, like the therapist had given me. I jumped online and began searching. After only a few minutes, I found some great articles on meditation. I hadn't really tried meditation before but the way my mind was going now, I thought it might be a good idea.

According to the article, humans cannot control the thoughts that enter our minds. We can only control our fixation upon them. Sounded good to me, I needed to stop this over-thinking. My logical brain was telling me Sarah simply had to work late. She seemed to understand and love me despite my struggles. I certainly loved her despite hers. The other side, the dark side, whispered every horrible fear. If I meditated and really learned to quiet that part of my brain, maybe it would help.

I put the first You Tube one up on the T.V. in the living room. I got into a comfortable position. I breathed in for four, held for four, and out for five. I concentrated on the music and a little bell that the guy rang every few seconds. My arms felt funny the way I held them up, so I changed put my palms down. I tried again. And again. And again.

After twenty minutes, I wondered if meditation was for me. I'd spent most of the minutes trying to focus on my breathing, trying to not worry about muscles cramping, and finally, what I was going to make for dinner. I got up and turned off the T.V. I went to the kitchen and took out some vegetables to begin chopping. I poured myself a small glass of wine. I began chopping and stirring and pouring until the entire house was filled with the scent of cooking dinner. I cleaned up my mess and set the table. A few weeks ago at this time, I would have rushed out the door to be picking them up. Jordan drove now though. He would be bringing them home any second.

I went to my room and pulled out some clean clothes. I decided to take a quick shower, maybe dress up a little. I hadn't done that in ages. I even hoped Sarah would notice. I got a little excited at the thought and stepped into the warm water. It wasn't until I was rinsing my hair that I realized I hadn't worried anymore, over Sarah coming in late. I stepped out and toweled off, coming face to face with my reflection.

I looked at that woman staring back at me. She looked a little different from a few weeks ago. Yes, I still had the stretch marks and my boobs were still dragging. But my shoulders were straighter. My eyes were shining more. When I first caught a glimpse, I had even been smiling. I dried off and did my hair.

When I got downstairs, the kids were already home, and Jordan was standing at the stove, breathing in the aroma of the cooking dinner. Chloe sat the table with Sarah.

"I thought you were working late," I whispered when I got to her, I wrapped my arms around her shoulders and kissed her face.

Straightening up, I said, "How was your guys' day?"

Dinner fed more than my physical body that evening. I sat close to Sarah and we each had several glasses of wine. I held her hand and stroked her hair while our children chatted about their day. I rubbed her thigh high, right where she liked best, beneath the table. I kissed her cheek. I asked the kids to clean up the table.

Sarah announced she was going to take a quick shower and, "Do you guys want to play a game after?" I followed her down the hall.

Once in our room, I shut the door.

"Jess, what is all this about?" she turned and looked at me.

I didn't say a word, just worked at unbuttoning her blouse, then her trousers. I pulled off my own shirt and kissed her lips. I worked my way down her body and finally, we ended up on our bed. I held myself over her, kissing her mouth, stroking her. I watched as she gave way to the magical mystery of female orgasm, lost in ecstasy for a few moments. Afterward, I curled up on her right, my head on her shoulder.

"I don't know where that came from, but it was nice," she whispered. She stroked my hair, "You're so beautiful, you have made my life worth everything."

Then she got up and showered.

12

As the weeks turned over, I made more and more time for the things I enjoyed. Each day, I walked. I read books on interesting subjects. I took short naps when I need them. I meditated.

The first few times I practiced meditation were just like the first. As I did them more, I got better and better. My mind was cluttered as always, but my ability to ignore the clutter grew. I was amazed at how much tension I lost in just a matter of weeks.

Today, I decided to meditate on healing my own soul. I sat down in my now comfortable meditation pose and began breathing. In and out. I allowed the music to calm my mind and applied focus to envisioning a healing light pouring over my body. I imagined it pouring into my body, filling up each cell with its healing light, then spilling into the next. At one moment, I caught myself thinking this was healing my body, not my soul, but I couldn't envision my soul. I decided to just go with what seemed to be working.

I allowed this light to fill me up, up right up to my head, to my brain. It worked its way into each cell until I pictured the exact middle of my brain, deep in its center. The light filled and poured surrounding the center. The center was hard. It reminded me of a coconut, it was hard and round. I could almost feel the hardness of the shell against my hands.

I held the light trying anything to break into that shell, but it would not break. Coming out of the trance, I felt amazing. I had more energy, I was happier, and I was pleased I had been able to sit for nearly an hour working on healing myself. I got up to make tea.

As the water heated, I wondered at what just happened, and at what just *didn't* happen. Using my energy, I'd envisioned a sphere of light right before me. It was warm and golden, and I gave more and more energy to it until it grew. I allowed that light to enter my heart center, spreading through my entire body, literally into each delicate cell of my being. I was slowly learning to love every part of me; that light proved it. I briefly wondered how long it would take to love that part of me that was hidden deep within my brain.

The next day, I woke up feeling more amazing than I could remember, at least not since we had the babies. I did my usual chores and errands and before I knew it, the day was finished, and Sarah was walking through the door. I greeted her with a kiss to her cheek. Lately, I had felt so close to her, more than any other time during our entire relationship. She didn't kiss me back, but headed straight to her favorite chair at the kitchen table.

"How was your day?" I asked, even though watching her, I could tell it had been difficult.

"It was fine, we are a little behind in one project, but it should get sorted before too long. I'll be fine," she didn't look in my direction. With her eyes down, she asked, "How is the depression?"

I was taken off-guard. She hadn't really asked me how I was doing and she'd never labelled what I was going through as "depression." She'd asked how I felt, if I had a therapist, what I was doing to help myself but never asked how "the depression" was.

I smiled and shrugged, "You know, each day, it *is* a struggle. I can't lie. I wake up not knowing how I will feel or if I will get down during the afternoon. I am doing better though. I can remind myself feelings come and go and even depression will go. I learned to medit—"

She cut me off mid word.

"So. Better then?" she was so abrupt, I asked what was really bothering her.

She shrugged her shoulders at me and looked me right in the eye, "I took our vows very seriously, Jess. I really did. I still do. This is really something though. I come home, never knowing if you are going to be here or not. I can't count on you to do much unless you want to. I honestly need someone here to do their share, get the kids ready and out, keep our home up, and for the past how many weeks, I just haven't been able to count on you. For anything." She sighed, "I am glad you are doing better. I guess everyone has their limits is all."

I was stunned. I'd no idea she felt this way. I tried not to cry. I honestly didn't know what to say to her. I looked at her, the woman I'd chosen to live my life with, the woman I admired so much.

"I come home, I think I have given us a great home, and before, you know, you had it all together. I get it all coming down, you might think I don't, but I do. I get not knowing what our next step will be or how to get on with the kids growing up. I have the same worries. I come home now and you might be smiling, you might not. Hell, sometimes, you aren't even here, you've gone for a walk or doing something for yourself. You don't bother to ask how I am or if I am struggling. You just keep doing you though. I can't keep up like this."

Again, I was stunned, I'd no idea she felt this way.

My disbelief was slowly turning though. "So, it was fine if you came home to a clean home, dinner, and kids done with their activities? Well, the thing is, Sarah, I wasn't. I wasn't okay with all that. All I did for years was serve you three. I know you appreciated it, but you never once thought how such a life was affecting me or what it was taking away. I can hardly recall things I once liked, or even really feel anything. I was so numb. You're dropping this on me now, just *now,* when I finally feel like I can breathe, like I can be me without any guilt?" I was so hurt and even though my voice was low, it was harsh, filled with emotion. I brushed a tear from my face.

All those years, all the sacrifice, I thought she had noticed. I thought she appreciated it. Now, I just wasn't so sure.

She sighed. She looked sad, "I just am having a hard time being everything for everyone. Surely, you can see that, Jess?"

"How could I miss it? I did that for years. Sorry it's such an inconvenience for you."

I was beyond hurt, there was no way to ignore this or allow her selfishness to just slide by. My hands were shaking.

I glared at her and she glared back.

"You know, Jess, I never called you out for that night, I never demanded you explain or apologize even. I just went on with life, trying to figure out what was bothering you. I am allowed to be tired. I am allowed these feelings, just as you are," her voice was soft.

I thought about what she was saying. The truth was I had never complained to her during our entire marriage. If she wanted to do something, see something or even pick dinners, I was more than compliant. I had willingly given away my opinions, my desires and now I was learning, I'd given away my marriage. I didn't know what to say.

We didn't talk to each other, not through dinner, not afterwards. Sarah slept on the couch.

I thought about our argument over the next few days, actually, I thought of little else. How could I think of anything else?

The thing is all I had been feeling surprised Sarah. After all, I had never complained, I never argued. We were viewed as the "perfect" couple. People knew our relationship was a sure thing. No one could ever guess I had been numb for the better part of my adult-life. I had never spoken up for myself, how could Sarah possibly guess how I was feeling, much less why? I was only learning for myself after weeks of focused attention.

I decided to surprise Sarah for lunch one day. I got the kids out the door. I packed our old picnic basket and I headed towards the city. I was excited to see my wife. It had been years since I had surprised her and just as long as our last picnic. I hit traffic but thankfully, I had left in plenty of time and even with the delay, I parked in front of her building just in time for her lunch.

I jumped out and paid the parking fee, my arms full of the basket. After just a few minutes, I saw my wife. She was dressed perfectly in dark trousers and a light blazer. Her hair gleamed in the sun. She stopped when she saw me, I saw her take in the scene. She loved picnics. She walked over.

"What is this?" she was always so direct.

"I miss you every day you go to work, I just wanted to show you that."

She didn't step close enough for me to kiss her cheek or take her hand. She did start in the direction of the park though and I fell in step with her. She tucked her hands in her pockets. We didn't talk on our way, but we found a nice place to spread the blanket.

I set the basket down and pulled out the blanket. Sarah helped me spread it on the ground. We settled in and I pulled out our lunches.

"I've been thinking," I began, "I can see understand how you might believe my unhappiness is your fault, or that I have been lying to you through the years. I really do love our life and I wasn't unhappy. The truth is much more complicated than all that."

"When we met, I knew, without any doubts, you were the woman I wanted to be with my whole life. I wanted children with you and I wanted to grow old with you. I couldn't understand or even accept you felt the same way about me," I took a deep breath, this hurt to acknowledge how worthless I'd felt for such a long time, "I never felt worthy to be by your side, to call myself your wife. My therapist asked if I'd been jealous of you. I don't think I was, not like envious of how beautiful or smart you are. I just didn't accept someone like you could love me." I wasn't looking at her while I spoke, I was looking around, trying to articulate my thoughts.

"Then, you continued working, you've done so much better than I could ever have imagined. I stayed with the kids. You have stayed so fit and beautiful and compared to me, you've just done so well. I didn't feel worth this wonderful life, so I tried to make up for it. I served you three without ever asking for anything in return. I didn't ask to watch movies I wanted or pick out most dinners so you guys could get what you wanted. I was not loving myself and I couldn't accept your love, not fully, not while I was in that state," my voice caught,

"I never meant for this to hurt you, or the kids though. I never thought I would break like I have done."

I reached for her hand. I finally dared look over at her.

I was surprised to see her wiping tears off her face, "I didn't know you were doing all that. It sounds daft, now, because we have spent most days together for a long time. I never noticed. I just thought you were doing what you wanted. I love you. I love the sacrifice you made to carry our beautiful children. I love the fact that they have always had you to call if they needed. I love how you keep up our home and make all those dinners. I love that you don't need to compete with me. I love seeing you when I walk through the door."

"I was so afraid that night. I couldn't believe what they were telling me, how you were unconscious in the bathroom because you took some pill. I couldn't believe it, then I saw you. You were so helpless, your arms wide open, your legs crossed over each other when they picked you up to put you on the stretcher. I was so afraid you wouldn't wake up. Then you did, and I didn't know how to help. I couldn't make you better. I wanted to tell you how horribly you would be missed, how the kids were so afraid. I wanted to tell you how I watched over you, checking on your breathing all that first week you were home. I wished I could just tell your brain or thoughts or whatever was making you think the way you were how wrong they were. I loved you more than anything. I still do."

"I can't keep guessing though. If it is me, just tell me. If you want to do something, tell me. If you need a walk, go. I don't think you have to get a job, if you want, great, get one, but I do think you need something every day to do. I want that for you, now the kids are grown. I want so many things for us."

She was really crying.

I looked at her, "I just want to feel like I really matter. I want to believe myself when I tell myself those words. I was so hurt, you decided to *retire* without ever asking me."

She nodded, "I figured that out after a little while. I thought I could surprise you. I want to travel for a few months, just like we planned, right after I retire. I want to go somewhere new and discover it with you. I thought I would surprise you, but I figured out, at least, I think I figured out, what you might be thinking."

She gripped my hand tighter.

"All these years, you have been literally following or herding us around. I know your days were so busy, then slow, then busy as we all left for school and work and came home again. I wasn't thinking how that might have changed you or what you might want after all that. I was only thinking what we planned when we first got married. Remember? We were going to retire young enough to enjoy life, to make a difference. We were going to travel and live in hotels for a while. I saw my chance to leave work and do all that with you, so I took it."

I looked at her, I'd forgotten we had made those plans. We had our family and they were and to a large extent, still are my primary focus. I had such focus on our children, our family, I'd forgotten what made me *me*, but I had also forgotten what made us *us*.

I'd forgotten she always wanted to bring to her first military station in Korea. I wanted to travel the major rivers in Europe. I'd forgotten how we'd made those plans. She had not. I was touched.

I looked at her, "I'm sorry, that is all I can say. I am so sorry. I'm sorry I let myself go to that point, to that point of sheer exhaustion of living. I am sorry I forgot what you and mean. I think when you're in the trenches, all you see is what is right in front of you. More than that though, once you lose the bigger perspective, you get comfortable like that. You just get so complacent your life becomes simply doing what is right before you because that is all you see. For some reason, I became so used to that, I just forgot to look up. You are telling me you were retiring in a year, meant I had missed out on living some big parts of life. I certainly could never retire, much less at the ages we are right now. I have worked hard for our family but the idea that you provided all this while I numbly folded laundry and cleaned became so vivid that image overtook all others. I never measured up to you, and then I just was so dependent on you I couldn't bear the thought. I couldn't bear the thought that was why were still with me or that I'd allowed that somehow. Something just snapped and I couldn't see anything but backwards, nothing was before me." I was crying, really blubbering but I needed her to know, "I'm going to miss Jordan and Chloe so much, I can't even breathe when I think of them growing up. My days have revolved around them and their needs for so long, I am so afraid of just sitting all day, alone and unneeded. I am afraid to be alone, I never had to think about me before, I was so busy. I think the past few weeks have been wonderful healing time for me, but it has taken so much work to try and love myself."

She stroked my hand and didn't say anything for a little while.

It was nice, sitting there, together in the sunshine. I felt so safe when I was with her. Even though she hadn't noticed every single sacrifice I'd made each day for so long, she had held onto other precious things. She hadn't been content to simply wait out the kids growing up or just doing each little chore in front of her. She'd dare to look around and see what more she could do, see a wider perspective of how we could do all we'd set out to do.

"You know, Jess. I couldn't have done any of this life without you by my side. It's true. I never would have known the joy of being a mom. The nice parts of my day were all because of you. You never just cooked, you made memorable, nourishing meals that fed our family. Our home is gorgeous because you just know how to make it so. I would have worked myself into an early grave never knowing how nice a real home is."

I looked at her, it was hard to believe the amazingly put-together woman across from me was telling me her life was good because of me. "It's true," she assured me, "I would never have taken the time nor the effort to put such beauty in my life. And you know, that is what has made life worth living. I come home to a beautiful home and family. I eat wonderful things because you made them that way. Our children know the value of living well and caring for their things because of you."

We stayed in the park most of the rest of the afternoon. She called off work and walked me back to our car arm-in-arm. We drove home.

I couldn't help thinking what surprises life has in store for us. For such a long time, I'd just accepted my false belief system about myself; worse, I believed Sarah felt the same. I had convinced myself to believe the worst and those beliefs had robbed me of years of deep fulfillment, peace, and even, happiness.

When we got home, I told Sarah, "I am never going to be a warrior. I am never going to be famous. I haven't practiced the skills necessary to become a high earning partner in some firm. There are so many things I will never be and I fear, deep in my soul, that is not enough for you."

Sarah answered with a hug and whispered, "Those are your fears. You have to believe me when I tell you, you have made my life."

I held on to her, wanting to believe her. I knew she never lied to me. Why were these words so difficult for me to accept about myself? I thought I had been doing so well on my path of recovery. I couldn't believe her words though.

It was just like doing my light meditations, there was a part of me that was so hard-shelled, encrusted;

the light either could not or would not enter. I could hear her words, I could feel them, yet that little part of me that refused to accept her love also refused complete recovery.

Awareness is always the first step towards growth. I supposed I was happy that at the very least, I was aware of what I was facing. I felt as if I were behind a pane of glass, looking at all the life before me. I could see the beauty of it before me. The grass was lush and green. There were trees waving in a cool breeze. The sun was out and shining so brightly on the world just out of my reach. I could see people laughing and cheering. I could see it, but I was numb to the feelings such a scene produced.

Meditation brought presence, presence brought awareness, and awareness prompted growth. One day, I decided to simply take stock of the journey born from my recklessness. Once again, I was face-to-face with that woman in the mirror.

I no longer dreaded her appearance. I decided that fact was significant progress. I looked her over and another realization occurred; the image, though not dreaded, was not much changed. I still had the sagging breasts, the mum-tum, and my thighs could be smaller. Overall, I wasn't much smaller, my hair was the same cut, but I was standing taller. My shoulders were pulled back and up, stretching my back skywards and tilting my chin upwards. A small change but an admirable and measurable one.

I toweled off and leaned closer to the mirror. My eyes were a little wider, a little brighter. I decided, looking into those eyes, there hadn't ever been much to dread from this image. Just thinking that, slowed my breath and relaxed my shoulders. I dressed and dried my hair.

I sat in the center of my room to do my afternoon meditation. I called upon the light that I had so recently grown to love and rely upon. As it entered my heart, I felt its warmth spread throughout my entire being, filling me up, and spilling into the room. I concentrated and breathed, holding that light as powerfully and long as I was able.

I sat there and thought of how much my life had changed during the past few weeks. I no longer woke feeling tired or dreading the demands of the day. I didn't avoid my own reflection.

Only two changes, seemingly small, but living with them was unbearable. I felt my chin tremble at what was now only memory. I allowed this hurt to envelope over me, feeding that healing light. I felt tears slide down my cheeks, but I held my pose. My shoulders shook at the pain I'd felt but never allowed to service and the healing light turned bright blue.

I felt cold, then warm, and the light bluer and bluer. I sat with the energy. Only twice before had I experienced such energy, when I'd given birth first to Jordan, then Chloe. Through the hours of pain, my body produced two pristine babies. This energy differed a little, it felt more healing rather than producing. Years of pain now born unbreakable self-love. In those few moments, I felt as if I were one with the universe, completely capable of understanding the most existential questions all mortals face. For those few moments, I felt God.

I recalled with remarkable clarity, almost hearing Sarah's voice, as if shew were in the room, wishing I could feel how I'd made her life so wonderful. I believed her. I took in her words like lightning bolts. They streaked through me, finally bursting that hard-shelled space hidden deep in my brain causing it to ooze and leak stored self-hate. And I wept.

13

I didn't tell anyone about what I'd experienced during meditation that day. I went about my days, quietly happily. I'd felt such a strong shift, deep within my soul that day, allowing me to find true peace. It was nearly impossible to explain, the power of the energy I'd both produced and benefited from. The mystery of that day could only be understood through a *mantra* I had seen long ago and never understood until now, "God is as in me." I uttered those precious words almost constantly as I went through my days.

About a month after the meditation day, I read a small article on depression. A new brain mapping revealed depression often lies in wait in the very middle, towards the back of the brain. The place that I had envisioned, the place that refused me to truly heal, the place where that lightening energy finally struck, allowing me to find peace. My hands shook as I read the short article.

I tried to tell Sarah about both the experience and the article later that evening.

My voice was a little louder than normal, livelier, "I am telling you, I did the healing meditation over and again, it was like nothing could get that place to release until this day."

I looked at her, desperately wanting her to understand the significance of that day. I could see she would not.

I let the subject go. A few months ago, I'd desperately needed Sarah to understand me for me, to believe she loved me. I now accepted the fact that even though we are close, we are married, she lived a much different life. I hoped she would never encounter the crippling depression that so caged my living potential for so long, but I also knew if she did not, she could not truly understand the healing I'd experienced.

I kissed her on the cheek, "I love you," I whispered.

"And I, you," she held my hand, "I do think your experience is wonderful, Jess. I hope you know I don't mean to marginalize or trivialize that, I believe you. I guess I just can't quite think how something like that even takes place."

I believed her words, she meant them.

And she was right, she could never really understand. We were nearing her retirement day, it was only three months away. Nine months had passed since her original announcement. The same required time for human gestation.

The irony was not lost on me.

I had been re-born, or at the very least, been given a new chance to life.

Even though Sarah was not in the right frame of mind to understand my extraordinary healing, I thought of little else the next few days. There was no denying I felt stronger, both, physically and mentally, immediately following the meditation that day. I forgave Sarah for not understanding my garbled description of the experience and the article I could no longer locate. I could barely understand it myself.

I quietly contemplated that day, many times over, though trying to find some way to understand all I had gone through these past few months. I wrote out the journey on a time line.

'Sarah announced her upcoming retirement,' was number one.

Two, 'The realization how empty I'd felt for so long.'

'I tried to end the emptiness,' number three. I paused there and shuddered, recalling my frayed clothes and what I must have looked like in the bathroom. I moved on.

'The hospital,' I stopped at four.

So much had happened, I didn't enjoy reliving any of those things. They still hurt, I was still embarrassed. The hurt, the embarrassment did not halt me in my tracks, but it wasn't fun to contemplate those memories either. I tore up the paper.

Taking out a fresh sheet, I wrote a new list.

Realization.

Awareness.

Making Room.
Breathe.
Space.
Healing.

There, this list was much easier, much more comprehensive than my first attempt. Chloe interrupted my thoughts, "What's that, mommy?"

I showed her, "It shows my steps of the last few months, how far I have come. I decided to write this down, so I could really measure all I have done."

"Why?"

"Well, Chloe, that is a really great question. As you know, I suffered from severe depression."

Admitting this to my children was still difficult. I allowed for that difficulty by taking a deep breath, "I wanted to know exactly what I have done to heal from that."

"Is the depression gone?" her eyes were wide, hopeful. I was painfully reminded how difficult this journey had been for my family. I took another deep breath.

"You know, I don't know. I don't know if depression really goes away. I never have studied it. I can know, though, when it became unbearable pushing me to change or grow. I can understand that and I just feel like writing it down might help me or someone else later," I pointed to the first step, "I had to realize I needed to grow, I couldn't go on like I was. Life was too empty. That is where my journey really began. I realized and tried one change."

She nodded, I could see a darkness in her eyes as she recalled that horrible evening.

"You wrote down awareness next. Is that when you knew there might be another way?" her voice was quiet and she lovingly skirted around words such as "ending" or "suicide." I brushed her face with the back of my hand and leaned in to kiss her forehead. She rubbed away the kiss, like any other teen would making me smile a little.

"Yes, Chlo, I became very aware the next step was my choice."

I took in another breath.

"What came next?" she asked.

"I had to get rid of the things that held me back. I lost a few things, some old beliefs I'd held onto for too long. I don't believe anyone can exist, at least, not happily, between beliefs. I wanted something different and there just wasn't room for both," I explained best as I could. I didn't want to reveal everything and there was no reason to. I had raised Chloe to love herself, there was no reason for me to verbalize just how exhausting my lack of self-love had been; she'd waited for me to come home from the hospital after a suicide attempt.

"It was like I had to clear out a room that was full of old furniture. Then I had to really clean out that room. I opened the windows…"

"And you breathed in fresh air," she finished for me.

"Yes, that is exactly what I did. I made space, then I breathed in fresh air. I breathed in new life," I looked down at the list again, "I'd created space through losing my old beliefs. I had to fill it. And that is when my real healing began."

She nodded and didn't ask any more questions. I watched her as she left the table, stopping at the fridge for a snack. I hoped I had raised her to be strong enough to overcome life's obstacles. I looked at my list again. It looked so simple, just a few words to track and describe all I'd lost and gained in just a few months. Chloe kissed my cheek on her way out the kitchen, leaving me to my own thoughts about the list.

I stared at it for a few more minutes, then focused on the window overlooking the backyard.

I certainly had lost a lot this year, I thought. I lost all self-loathing that I had harbored but not acknowledged for far too long. Thanks to the memory regression, I could still recall with clarity the day I'd learned to think so poorly of myself. The memory still evoked some hurt, but I felt more powerful understanding that was no fault of my own.

Through that memory, I was also able to clearly see all I'd done for my own children. Life would be difficult for them. That was life. I had done my best to ready them to give them enough love to journey out on their own. I believed I had done this well, they were unafraid of most new situations, gracefully assessing each one and addressing each appropriately. They were so far ahead of where I'd been at their ages. I allowed myself a few moments to take pride in all the sacrifices that were now paying off as my children grew ever-towards their own adulthoods.

Through that pride, I'd lost the crippling fear of my own next chapter. My children would grow, that was simply the way of life. I didn't want to stop them and anyway, I couldn't. Life just doesn't work that way. I lost that crippling fear, gaining confidence in my next chapter. I no longer feared it and I even looked forward to it a little.

Sarah reminded me of all we once dreamt and how we could now plan for those dreams. My confidence had led me to lose the belief I wasn't good enough for my wife. I gained her love on a deeper level than I ever thought attainable. It was a strange circle. I accepted and loved myself. I gained confidence and lost fear. I could then accept Sarah's love fully without challenge. Just thinking this warmed my entire being a little.

I could accept I was good enough for her. I could accept all I had done was enough. I only get one life; with a numbered amount of days and hours, giving me time enough to do many great things but not all. I didn't have to do all, what I *had* done was both good and enough. My life had been amazing, filled with much love. I could now accept I didn't have to suffer to experience the life I was given. I had worked hard for it and that was enough. Through some luck or fate, I had found Sarah but all that came after had been won through work.

I thought back to a friend who accused me once of being too privileged. She had only known me a short while after I'd had children. We never talked about our childhoods or how we'd met our spouses. We never spoke of life before our children. We never spoke of the work a good marriage takes or how much sacrifice is so often demanded of a parent. Her words hurt me and yet, they were empty and held no truth.

I didn't have to prove myself, I didn't have to prove my background. All I had to do was live. My life was enough.

Now a year after Sarah retired, I reflect on the life I was given. I still hope I earned that precious gift, grew with it, and evolved as much as I could. I am happy though, finally at peace with the ideas I learned along the way.

I still get down, but now, I give those moments their space and breathe through them. Sometimes, that space requires days and even though that is so difficult, I know I can do it. Everything has changed from what I knew and I give that space, too.

Jordan decided to graduate early and moved out that summer. I thought my heart would break as I watched him drive away, honking his horn, smiling, and waving. I wanted to hang onto the bumper of his car and beg him to stay. I didn't and my heart didn't break. I am at peace with him exploring life on his own.

Chloe is driving. She went out with her first boyfriend. Sarah handles the first love bites well, probably better than I did. I thought my children growing up would hurt and I always feared "that day." I am at peace though. I am so glad they explore life and find what they like and don't like. I am glad they are jumping in with both feet.

Sarah retired and for the first few months, we did just as we'd planned. We traveled. We stayed in nice places. We saw the sights. We came home. I thought

Sarah would next start some big ambitious community project but I was wrong.

Sarah found she enjoyed being home. She loved waking up and going for a run or walk. She worked in the garden. She read and she decided that was enough. I was the one who stepped out and began spear heading community projects.

I was surprised. I have never given speeches before, never presented to crowds. The more I have done, the more I have enjoyed. Gone are the days of terrible loneliness and silence filled hours of waiting for someone to need me.

I miss my old life, the previous chapters. I miss my babies. I even miss some of the free time. I lost those things through living. I have gained some incredible, hard-won gifts that I never dared dream possible for too many years. I love myself. Deep down, I love me. I share that love with others and accept theirs in return. My relationships with my little family have only grown and strengthened through that love. I miss my babies but I love the people they have grown into and it is certainly less work. I miss my pre-baby body, but I love that I experienced creating another human.

As for Sarah and me, our marriage, our relationship, our love for each other has deepened. Once I became aware of all my insecurities, my own self-hate, and lost those, I gained a true appreciation for the woman who dared spend her life with me. I had no idea how much peace I was missing out on, simply because I never knew how to love myself. As I accepted her love fully, I am able to return it fully.

www.ingramcontent.com/pod-product-compliance
Lightning Source LLC
Chambersburg PA
CBHW060452310726
48977CB00001B/404